THE SCENE OF THE MURDERS

Jane followed Davis, room by room, looking at everything, taking mental snapshots as they went. The worst thing to see was the nursery. Diane Flock had already begun stenciling scenes from *Winnie the Pooh* and *Peter Rabbit* along the pale blue walls. A crib, barely out of the box, was in the corner. On the walls, pictures of Grandma and Grandpa, and friends, and Mommy and Daddy. A stroller, still in the box, up against the walk-in closet's door. Two or three baby shower gifts on the windowsill, still wrapped. It made her want to weep when she saw this. Knowing what she would find next.

In the master bedroom she found it.

"I told you to be prepared," Davis said.

"I am," Laymon lied....

NIGHT CAGE

ANDREW HARPER

LEISURE BOOKS   NEW YORK CITY

LEISURE BOOKS ®

November 2004

Published by

Dorchester Publishing Co., Inc.
200 Madison Avenue
New York, NY 10016

ISBN 0-8439-5288-1

The name "Leisure Books" and the stylized "L" with design are trademarks of Dorchester Publishing Co., Inc.

Printed in the United States of America.

Visit us on the web at www.dorchesterpub.com.

For Jane Osnovich

With thanks to my co-conspirator, Raul Silva.
Additional gratitude to my editor, Don D'Auria;
thanks also to Steve, and to Matt.

Visit www.DardenState.com to find out more
about Andrew Harper and his novels.

NIGHT CAGE

Tyger, tyger, burning bright
In the forests of the night
What immortal hand or eye
Could frame thy fearful symmetry?

—William Blake

PROLOGUE

Now

October was hell, and he knew it was because of the wind itself.

The Santa Ana winds blew down like the roar of a lion along the arroyos and canyons of the desert; across the mountain passes into the bowl of valley known, depending on which county you were in, as San Bernardino, Riverside, and San Pascal, all sharing the dry October of Southern California, too far inland from the ocean to get a cool breeze, too far from the desert to thrive in the heat. The mountain pass beneath Big Bear was blocked off by the fires that had spread along the ridge. Below this, the foothill communities, and across the flatlands of freeway and neighborhood grids, pre-dawn, a ridge of hills that seemed nearly prehistoric with their red rock and sporadic sprays of palm trees. Heat and dust coughed through the air, and the young man who felt them most, who was choked by a chilling terror at the shadows that flew by night, lay staring up at the window, listening to it rattle with the wind.

Those burning winds brought the shadows to him. Blew them all back from the edge of hell or heaven.

Night fears.

Fingers coming toward him, scraping at his throat.

The night fears grew with darkness, and they were like the shadows he saw sometimes, moving toward him, reaching for him. He could barely breathe when they touched his skin, and he lay awake all night waiting for the faintest light through the window.

Then the light slowly came up from outside; he heard her get out of bed in the next room and go run the shower in the bathroom. Still sleepy. Not ready to get up. Just another hour or two of sleep. Another dream before the day had to get going.

He called himself Doc, although he hadn't yet cured himself of the night fears that came on unexpectedly. Still, he knew how to heal, set limbs, and make infections go away. But the night fears were always after him, and he had slept poorly yet again. Sometimes, he didn't fall asleep until the rest of the world awoke. In all his nineteen years, he could not remember a good night of sleep. The night fears came in the dark, and they crawled all over his skin, kept him from drifting into the dreamworld he wanted to find. But by the time of the first light outside the window, he knew he was safe after all. Even in his bed, his special bed, he knew the night fears could not get him.

But it was the purple light outside the window that relaxed him the most. The white hot light of midday hurt him. The dark of night brought the fears crawling to him.

But early mornings and twilight were just perfect times.

He curled up into as much of a ball as he could make of himself. His arms hurt, as they often did, but he felt that warmth of happiness in this position.

His special bed.

The cage.

The crate was just large enough for him to scrunch himself into, and just tall enough that he didn't press against the top of it. He felt good in the cage, and more importantly, he felt safe, at least until she returned each day to take him out of it. The night fears couldn't get in there with him. It was just big enough for him and no one else.

His early memories of the cage, from the time he was four, were calming and sweet and allowed him to sleep at night without fear. Sometimes, she brought fear with her, like a smell on her. She didn't always shake it off at the door, as she promised. She sometimes brought rage with her, too, and then he didn't mind being locked into the cage.

Sometimes after she'd let him out, she would tell him about his father, and where he'd been conceived, and how it was like an enormous cage itself. He liked her best when this happened.

He liked to hear her memories of that place with its special rooms and all the people she talked about, and how she described his father to him. "He was a good

3

man then," she said. "But he made promises. And he broke some of them. He made some things terrible for me. And for you. But everyone who breaks a promise pays a penalty in life. You know that, don't you? Someday you'll get to meet him. Someday he'll find you, or you'll find him. Someday he'll pay the penalty for what he's done. Punishment always comes to people, whether in this life or the next. And the punishment always fits the crime."

In the cage, curled up in a ball, he fell asleep just as the sun was coming up beyond the room. He dreamt of the place where his mother and father had met, as if it were a promised land to which he'd one day return.

It was a hospital. He felt he knew the place by memory—just from what his mother had told him. About the high fences with the wires made out of razors. About the police everywhere. About all the doctors, all as smart as he was, as smart as his mother. The long corridors of rooms with windows in the doors so patients could look out. In his dreams, he felt he floated down the corridor and saw the people staring through their door-windows, watching him as he went, ghostlike, to find the cage where his mother had lived when his father had made love to her.

Even in the dreams, he saw the words emblazoned on the sign as he passed along the outside wall of one of the buildings:

THE DARDEN STATE HOSPITAL FOR CRIMINAL JUSTICE.

PART ONE

PART ONE

CHAPTER ONE

Discharge papers for Mary Chilmark, 1984
The Darden State Hospital for Criminal Justice

The patient expressed on more than one occasion remorse for the torture and murder of the three patients under her care while she was a registered nurse. Although she still maintains that the fire in the ward was an accident, and therefore two of the deaths were accidents, she admits that she did not then fully have the capacity to understand her actions in the matter. She understands that the fire had begun because of her own actions. She expressed great remorse and evinced anguish over what she had done.

In the current interview, the patient was fully oriented. She was calm, and expressed remorse for her past crimes. She understood the full importance of what the word "murder" meant, and expressed a moral view and judgment of her own actions in the past. She stated that she had suffered depression and anxiety, exacerbated at the time by drug and alcohol use, precipitated by the death of her parents (in 1974). "I got to the groups, including the PARTNER meetings and the MOVE group sessions. My individual sessions have proved more than satisfactory with Dr. Brainard."

When asked about the offense, she stated, "I know that I committed those murders, but I could not see this for several years. I suppose the part of me that had no mental control believed I was doing them good. But I know now how tragically wrong that was." She has internalized blame, as has been noted since October 1983. She does not view others as causing her maladaptive behavior, and she appears in every respect willing to take responsibility for her behavior.

Remission Status: Is the patient's severe mental disorder treatable by medication and psychological as well as social support avenues?

Robert Brainard: Extreme progress with this patient. Her functioning level is high, and has been instrumental in the "Patient In-Care" Reach in Wards B and C. The treatment team assessed her as in the top functioning category, and she had family support beyond the walls of Darden State. Her hallucinations from intake until spring 1984 were frequent and delusional. These might have been after-effect flashbacks to her prescription drug addiction, and seem to have cleared up completely.

The patient's severe disorder is completely in remission, and has seemed so for more than 18 months.

Level of Danger: Does the patient represent a substantial or implicit physical harm to others based on disorder or past history?

RB: As demonstrated by the past 18 months of observation and inquiry, no. In my opinion, and the opinion of the treatment group, Mary Chilmark is ready to transition back into the community.

Outpatient Treatment: What is recommended to continue the patient's treatment?

RB: Psychiatric treatment should be continual, and the state's supervision of this treatment is implicit. However, the patient is ready for the challenges and rigors of the outside world. She has the support of her fiancé, and his family, as well. Additionally, her pregnancy seems to be a mitigating factor, and I strongly recommend Mary Chilmark be given a second chance at this point in time. With outside supervision, continuing treatment by a state-appointed psychiatrist, continuing medical supervision, parenting classes, and ongoing medications as listed in the previous report, she should be out of the hospital and will not pose a threat, significant or otherwise, to the world at large.

Control Factor: What is the nature of the patient's past crime, and the original diagnosis?

RB: The murders of two women, one man, and an unborn child. Each murder seemed to have an element of irony, for they were people who, in her original state, the patient felt had done some moral or spiritual wrong that needed to be "brought back to them tenfold." Original diagnosis: narcotic-induced hallucinatory aggressive disorder, psychotic affective disorder, religious mania, depression, seizures (as illustrated in her MRI), and post-traumatic stress syndrome. But these seem to have been temporary in nature, owing much to the stress of her occupation (nurse) and the death of her father at the onset of her breakdown. Her depression and anxiety have been successfully managed for 18 months with medication therapy.

CHAPTER TWO

Now
October
1

She had a face like love itself. That's what he thought whenever he looked at her. Late forties, but could pass for thirty-two on a sunny day. Maybe even twenty-eight. She was prettier than any girl he had ever known. Her eyes were warm and brown, but had flecks of light in them like cinnamon, and her forehead was low but hidden by sweeps of raven-dark hair. Her name was Mary, and she had been a nurse all her life, with the exception of the handful of years lost to a hospital where she'd stayed after her breakdown. But in her face, anyone could see that her conscience was clear, her mind her own, and she moved and spoke as if each step she took was methodical and controlled. She was a gift to life.

And she kept the fears away.

Doc trusted her completely.

11

She shifted the curtain slightly, and bright sunlight entered the room. "Look at it out there," she said, so softly that he barely heard her. "It's beautiful."

He set down the instrument he'd been testing, and stepped over to the window. Mary stepped away and left him gazing outside as if it might relieve some of the anxiety he was feeling.

"Just an ordinary day," she said, going over to where the instruments were kept in a neat row on a napkin-covered plate.

Outside, the pure flat light of a Southern California October, dappled by the palm trees and the two enormous avocado trees at the edge of the back lawn by the guesthouse. Beyond, the swimming pool that was blue and lovely.

"Too much light," he said. "Too bright."

"But it's good in here, isn't it?" she said.

"The dog's barking," he said. "I wish it would just stop."

"Block it out," she said. "Doc, you need to concentrate."

"It's distracting."

"You're letting it do that. Come away from there. Ignore it. Focus."

He let the shades drop—the curtains were thick and too dark for such a room. His hand felt greasy; he had begun to sweat, which sometimes happened. He had to calm himself. *You can do this. You can do it.*

His heart seemed to pound in his chest. His mouth, dry. His mind focused, yet aware of the sensations that had begun.

The excitement.

The examination room: not sterile enough. He would have to deal with less-than-optimal conditions. He washed his hands with antibacterial soap, but still he felt dirty. He looked to her face for a sense of calm. She had it. Her skin was lightly tanned, and even though he saw the creases of age in her face—around her eyes and at the edge of her lips—he couldn't help feeling just a little better from seeing those deep brown eyes of hers.

"Don't worry," she said. "It's all right. When this is over, you'll be fine. We'll clean up, and you'll see. You'll see. She'll be better, too."

"I don't like this," he kept saying.

His left hand trembled. He looked at it, hoping to calm it just by taking deep breaths.

"It can't be helped." She stood by, her hands cupping the small metal basin to catch the blood. Surgery of this type was never a perfect option. But when a need arose, and the question became life and death for the mother and child, a good doctor had to be prepared to work even under the most rudimentary conditions.

In this case, that meant the master bedroom of a suburban house, while the woman on the bed stared at them, her eyes wide. Noises came from her mouth.

He could turn her off in his mind. Good doctors could do that. There was no time for anesthetic, and his assistant—who was nearly a doctor herself—tied the woman's arms so that when he brought the blade down to her belly to help with the removal of the child, the path would not be obstructed.

The woman's mouth had been taped, but only for her own good. She would pass out from the pain, or her body would take over, knowing this was for the good of the child inside her.

Nature was like that—it was both healer and caretaker. Her body would begin to divert the signals of pain to her brain so as to release the body's own natural painkiller.

The doctor prepared the woman's belly, and cut, and opened. He felt inside her for the tumor.

He glanced up at his assistant. "I can't find it."

His assistant—who was also his mother—raised her eyebrows. Her face had been spattered with blood.

"The baby," he said. "It's not here."

"Of course it's there, Doc."

"No," he said, feeling around within the cut.

"We need to get her to the hospital right away, Doc," his mother said.

"I think it's too late for that," he replied. "Let's close her up."

"No," his mother said. "See? She's just sleeping. She'll pull through. Here. I can feel her pulse. She'll be fine. She's still there. I can feel her. She hasn't passed yet."

His mother put her hand on the woman's sweat-soaked forehead, then reached down to tear the duct tape from her mouth.

That's when Doc thought he saw a shadow pass across the room, and he whispered something about how souls moved at death. He didn't mention the dark spiders he saw crawling off the woman's hand—the tiny little spiders of fear that stayed behind.

He didn't have to mention them.

He hoped he could leave the room without coming too close to them.

Later, in the dark of their own home:

"I saw her pass," he said.

"Did she say anything, Doc?"

"She told me that it was all right. She thanked me. You, too."

"Ah. I thought she might. She understands."

"She had her baby with her, too. She was going toward a light."

"They do that. Were there others with her? Beings of light?"

"She smiled at me," he said, and his mother's hand stroked his hair softly.

"Were there others?" she asked.

"I think so. I'm not sure. I saw shadows."

"They're shadows if they can't pass to the other side. They stay here. Did you see the fears?"

He nodded. "But I didn't go near them."

"I'll always keep them away from you. I promise."

"There were some light shadows and some that were darker than dark," he said. "And then, once she left, the light faded. I think she wanted to go."

"You're a good doctor," his mother said. "All those books on surgery really taught you a lot. It's amazing what you can do, Doc."

She drew him out of his cage.

"Don't ever leave me," he whispered, and then his mother pressed her lips against his slightly parted mouth.

CHAPTER THREE

1

The San Pascal murder lottery, as the homicide division's staffers liked to call it, usually hovered at under twenty per year, but the one that happened that afternoon put them just over, and if you counted the baby, it was twenty-three, even though they hadn't found the baby yet.

In the soft-focus neighborhoods of the foothills, with the beautiful homes, expansive lawns, and long pale blue swimming pools, murder of this type usually could be kept at bay by extensive alarm systems and the patrolling cars of off-duty policemen who were hired to notice unwelcome and uninvited visitors. At least, that was the myth. While there had been three suicide attempts in the area within the past six years, seven arrests regarding domestic violence, and one very suspicious crib death, murder had not walked these particular streets for at least thirty years.

Homeowners often owned at least one firearm, and

the Neighborhood Watch program was in full effect, run by a man named Mr. Moulton, who walked his Corgi three times daily along four of the streets. Mr. Moulton made stained glass, which was popular with the neighbors, in the home studio which had once been a guest house at the back of his property. Alanna Rogers, whose passion was gardening ever since her early retirement from Jet-Propulsion Laboratories, also was often in her front yard, tending to the maze of color and blossom. She had noticed when the small blue truck had come through, loaded with yard workers. She had noticed when a strange man had stared too often up to the window of the Mills' daughter's bedroom for it to be healthy, and, thinking of that Elizabeth Smart girl and how she had been kidnapped in some other state, she had notified the police about the man.

Others in the neighborhood felt they were well aware of the comings and goings of nearly everyone, from the young man who regularly bicycled through the neighborhood wearing very little other than Speedos and sneakers, to the three Goth-looking teen girls who seemed to sweep through on autumn afternoons, smoking and snickering, and picking flowers at will from perfectly nice gardens of homes that were not theirs.

But no one had seen the murderers that late October day.

The Flock house had its two cars in its driveway. Mr. Flock—rarely called Dan by the neighbors because he and his wife had never really mingled since they'd moved in two years earlier, buying the enormous house at earthquake-sale prices—worked for one of the studios in Los Angeles, although no one in the neighborhood was sure if it was Disney or Universal. He worked in the finance department, and had done well for himself in a short period of time.

Diane Flock was better known because she walked their golden retriever in the early evening, and sometimes, when she was up by the golf course, several blocks away, she ran into others out on their jogs or walks, and talked about the water problems or the earthquake damage from too many years back that still affected the houses, or about how someone had lost their beloved cat to a coyote. She worked at a law firm downtown, but had been going part time since she'd become pregnant, and was looking to leave the firm and "become just like my mother—someone who gets to be home all day. I'll go insane, I know it," she had told Phyllis Sherman, when picking up dog poop in a plastic bag near the entrance to the canyon-park area, just beyond the neighborhood.

The doors to the house had all been locked from the inside, although Diane Flock sometimes left the sun porch door open when she was home. The pool had been emptied because of some damage found. Apparently, that day she had stepped down into it and looked along the crack that ran from the bottom middle all the way up to diving board.

Because she'd left Molly, their golden retriever, in the dog run out by the three olive trees that ran along the back fence of the property, the dog had been spared her masters' fate.

"We heard her barking," Mr. Moulton told the police

later. "But she barked all the time. That was the one complaint everyone had about the Flocks. That dog."

"They had exquisite taste," Alanna Rogers said. "They bought their furniture at the big shows at the Pacific Design Center. They had antique dealers come to them. It must have been inherited, some of that wealth. They were such a beautiful couple. So blessed."

Within the house, tiny pencil writing on the wall, above the gold paisley sofa:

Diseased.

A hypodermic needle on the Stickley table near the front door.

On the Mission bench, in the enclosed, shaded sun porch, a scalpel with the brown of dried blood and the smallest of hairs upon it.

A stained-glass window set into the kitchen door, a smudge of blood against amber.

In the kitchen, the phone, dropped on the Mexican tile floor. Beside it, a broken vase. Three purple irises that had been picked from the garden the morning before.

In the upstairs hall, a bit of a cotton shirt, torn, with microscopic skin fragments in it where someone had used their fingers to tear the shirt from one of the victims.

In the second-floor bathroom, the shaving kit on the back of the toilet, open. The small window slanted to allow air. The medicine cabinet's mirrored sliding doors pushed to one side. In it, Crest toothpaste, Shower to Shower deodorant powder, a small vial of liquid foundation, a plastic bottle of Neutrogena facial moisturizer.

Razorblades on the light blue fuzzy rug beside the sink.

A deodorant bar on the floor.

A surgical mask, just to the left of the toilet, almost behind the small wicker trash basket.

In the trash basket, latex gloves.

Down the hall, along the expensive Persian runners, bought on a trip to Morocco in 1998, a sliver of fingernail caught in the fabric. In the master bedroom, the victims.

In pencil, tiny writing, just above the headboard on the wall:

Tumor, malignant, removed.

2

The house was in a small web of neighborhoods off Hill, a long street that went up into the gently rounded slope of hills in San Bernardino, California. This neighborhood was old and haughty, and had beautiful homes and a wide stream that ran down beside it off in the coyote wash just the other side of the houses along the rim of the hill, near the fire break. Beyond the foothills, there was a fire up on the mountains, just beneath Big Bear and Arrowhead. The Santa Ana winds shifted hourly, but so far the fire had not spread down into the foothill communities, which seemed unaffected by the smoke thousands of feet above their streets and swimming pools.

A brief street turned off Hill, and then another came down, called Minuet. Detective Jane Laymon glanced along the ivied lawns and richly textured gardens of the area. Jane was in her mid-twenties, but had jumped in rank since the previous winter, had qualified for her firearms, had begun working on more murder cases, much to the chagrin of her mother, who already disapproved of her relationship with a young man named Danny, and who told Jane that she needed to "stay away from all that killing." But Jane had begun to love the puzzles that built up around her work, and had become particularly fascinated with the work of the forensics experts in San Pascal, most of whom now were in this particular neighborhood.

The colors of summer had faded into the brown-dust of Southern California's fall—October was the fire month, and the hills above were red and brown, barely recovered from the previous year's fires that had swept down, threatening some of the houses in the area, destroying a large section of the hill's live oak and scrub. But you'd never know it in on these streets, just beneath the hills, for the gardens were well watered, and the greens of fruit trees and of blue jacaranda and crimson and white bougainvillea brought the memory of eternal summer with them. Palm trees grew along the curb, giant sentries to each of the large houses. Unlike other neighborhoods nearby, which often had one distinct type of architecture, each house here was completely different from the next: first an adobe, then a Portuguese-style mansion, then a wedding cake house, then a gothic Tudor mess, a Victorian pile, a plain blue bungalow, but peppered among these were a series of California Crafts-man homes. These had the dark wood construction, with beautiful, expansive porches with square columns supporting a low-pitched roof, and the wide eaves along the rooftop, providing shade along the side yard.

She found the house number, and pulled into the driveway of one of the craftsman houses. Rosemary hedges in front. Twin palm trees, thick and looming, on either side of the driveway. Jade plants, the height of a small child, untended, growing wild. A low apple tree in the front yard, as well as what looked like two pomegranates; their fruit, long past, lay in clumps along the spotty overgrown grass.

The forensics team had arrived there three hours before. Two SUVs were in the driveway. The police tape was up. Two cruisers parked just down the block. She parked her car at the edge of the long driveway and walked slowly up to the house.

3

"Laymon. Glad you came out for this." Marty Davis looked worn and tattered from lack of sleep, his hair a bit wild, and his eyes circled with dark smudges.

One of the other detectives, named March, glanced over at her. He was short and stout, and wore a starched white shirt stained at the armpits. He didn't say anything, but she felt some kind of criticism in the way he looked at her. Maybe it was her eye patch. The legend of her missing eye had gone far afield because the investigation of the Red Angel killer had become a big one in California. She went over to March, and he seemed a bit startled by this.

"Look, I lost my eye chasing a killer. Want to know what he did to get it? You want a good look at it?" She reached up to lift the patch, but March turned away.

"Laymon," Davis said. "We didn't bring you out here for your eye."

"What kind of consult are we talking about?" she asked, turning her attention back to him.

"It's a team effort. Come on," he said. He led her along the route that had been understood to be the blocking of the murders. "She's out here. Maybe there." He pointed to the empty pool. The sunlight out back seemed blinding. Jane shielded her eye. She squinted, trying to imagine a woman in that pool. "They had some damage. Already there when they bought the house, apparently. A crack at the bottom of the pool. They had tried repairing it since they moved in, but nothing worked. They bought the place in an earthquake sale. It should've gone for over a half a million, but it went for three hundred. The neighbors all felt it was scandalous to get this place that cheap."

"There's a guest house," Jane said, looking at the small blue house beyond the pool.

"Yep. A one bedroom. No occupants. Looks like they used it for storage."

"It's been checked?"

Davis nodded. "The pooch was in the dog run." He pointed to the chain-link rectangular area back among some trees.

"What time of day was it?"

"Not sure. Maybe mid-afternoon. I guess three. He gets home from work early on Fridays."

"So he came in while it was going on."

"Maybe," Davis said. "Come on, let's go."

4

Three cops were in the kitchen, just standing around.

"The techs already come through?"

One of the cops nodded, grinning. "Hey, Jane."

"Hey, Pete. You might want to clear this place a little," Laymon said.

"It's because it's unincorporated land up here," Davis said. "It's county, not city."

Jane knew: red tape. Too many departments to call.

Davis walked her around the broken glass on the floor. The flowers, drying out. "She was at the pool, looking around it, who knows. She comes back in the house. She cuts some flowers on the way. Those grow right by the backsteps to the sun porch. She gets this vase from there," he pointed to the sink. "And just as she puts the flowers in, someone grabs her. Or scares her. Or she hears a noise."

"Maybe," Jane said. "Was she messy?"

Davis glanced at her, a question forming.

"Some people drop things. And they think, 'I'll let someone else clean that up.' What if she just dropped it, and left it?" Jane asked. "It might have nothing to do with her murderer. Did she have a maid? A cleaning service? A gardener?"

"This is why I want you here," Davis said, beaming a little. He escorted her along the narrow hallway with its dark, elegant table. A grandfather clock near the front door. A portrait of a teenage girl on the other side of the door. "Nearest we know, that's one of the victims. When she was young."

The girl in the portrait had long dark hair, cut in a way that reminded Jane of the 1970s. She smiled, and had a peaches-and-cream complexion. The artist had been a good one. It looked expensive, and nearly museum quality.

"How old was she?"

"Late thirties."

"I thought she was younger."

"They were a young couple—meaning 'new.' Married four years. First pregnancy."

"She was pretty," Jane said, feeling a bitter sadness when she looked at the painting. It reminded her yet again that the victims of murder had once been someone's beloved children. While the murderer often perceived the victim as an object, a toy, a means to an end, the victim had a history, a life, a richness of experience, and dreams of the future as well as memories of the past. That was probably the worst thing about any murder. Thinking about the victim's life. Seeing all life within that dead body. All chances ended. All hopes gone.

"And here," Davis said, as they came upon the low Stickley table, "is where we found the needle. And over there—" he pointed to what looked like a blackened portion of the rug. "They tried to set a fire, I'm guessing. Didn't stay long enough to complete it.

Maybe it was to try to cover up the crime. Either way, it just died down—nothing caught. Maybe it was an accident. Who knows? I guess 'til we find 'em, we won't know."

5

Jane followed Davis, room by room, looking at everything, taking mental snapshots as they went. The worst thing to see was the nursery. Diane Flock had already begun stenciling scenes from Winnie the Pooh and Peter Rabbit along the pale blue walls. A crib, barely out of the box, was in the corner. On the walls, pictures of grandma and grandpa, and friends, and mommy and daddy. A stroller, still in the box, up against the walk-in closet's door. Two or three baby shower gifts on the window sill, still wrapped. It made her want to weep when she saw this. Knowing what she would find next.

In the master bedroom she found it.

"I told you to be prepared," Davis said.

"I am," Laymon lied.

6

After examining the scene of the murders carefully, she left the room and sat outside in the sun by the pool.

Davis followed her out and sat by the empty pool, his feet dangling over the edge. "I guess when you're middle-aged like me, you see enough of these that it doesn't hit you the same way."

"It's not that," Jane said. "I just felt a bad vibe up

there. I felt as if the killers were still in the house. I know they're not. But it felt like it."

"You're about what, twenty-five?"

"Twenty-six."

"You've been through a hell of a lot for twenty-six."

"I took the job to handle all this. Don't worry, I'm not cracking."

"Tryon thinks the world of you."

"That's good to know."

"I wish somebody had said this to me when I was about your age and getting into this line of work. Don't worry about it when it gets to you. It gets to all of us. You never quite get numb," he said.

"Thanks," she said. Then, her mood changing, "We got Dahl coming in on this?"

"He'll lead, and you and I and maybe Joe March'll be on this."

"The one fascinated by my eye patch."

"You're a legend. You have to accept it. Nobody here has that. They respect you. Believe me. They do."

"I hope we catch the people who did this," she said.

"We will," Davis said. "They're sloppy. And we got a great team working on it."

7

Less than twenty minutes later, the call came in that they'd caught one of the killers down at a pharmacy in town, trying to get the victim's prescriptions refilled.

That evening, Jane Laymon called Trey Campbell.

"A consult?" he asked.

"They're going to put him in Darden until the trial.

28

We can get Hannafin and Brainard on it, but I want you on it, too. We're not getting much from this guy. He's really a Darden case. Just out there. Talks about spiders coming to get him. His mother's Mary Chilmark. She's part of it. We just haven't gotten her."

"Oh," Trey said. "I haven't thought about her in years. I came in after she'd already left. She was sort of a legend here. I knew patients who talked about her. She was a beauty who walked in, used the system, and walked right out again."

"I guess she never quite got the cure," Laymon said.

"I really like to think that when someone gets released from Darden, it's for a good reason."

"Well, if the rumors of the kid's father were true, then maybe that's the good reason."

Trey didn't respond to this. "Was it a rough take down?"

"Six men, two women. All holding a nineteen-year-old on the floor near the vitamin display. He really spun out of control."

"What was the prescription for?"

"That's yet another weird part of all this. Sleeping meds, basically. He risked getting caught just for sleeping pills."

"Maybe he has trouble sleeping."

"Given what he did in that house, I hope he does."

"Anyone hurt?"

"A few bruised egos, but no real damage."

"That's good."

"He calmed down right away, once they had him pinned."

"When does the guy come in?"

"Tonight."

"I'll see him when I get in tomorrow, I guess."

"We're leaving it to Hannafin to sort out. But she knows that you're the one for intake. She squawked about that, but there's not much she can do. Brainard probably shut her up."

"What's his first name?"

"He goes by Doc."

"What's his real name?"

CHAPTER FOUR

1

At his home in Redlands, across the valley, Trey closed his cell phone. Trey Campbell had only recently turned forty and hadn't yet noticed age creeping up on him in any defining way. He felt as good as he had since as far back as he could remember. But he felt the years in one way: He now had basic fears about life that he hadn't had up to his mid-thirties. While he had been working with psychopathic killers at the Darden State Hospital for Criminal Justice since he was in his twenties, fresh from his studies in psychology, the effect of the terror that a man or woman in a psychotic state of mind could inflict upon others had begun to dig into him as it never had before. He had witnessed deaths and mutilations at the hands of a few of the worst killers that Darden State kept within its gates. He had seen the sorrow of victims—even of a child whose mother had been brutally murdered trying to save the boy.

And though he loved the work, and felt it presented a multitude of challenges that kept him on his toes and thinking and growing in some way—he had begun to feel genuine fear about life.

Despite this, cell phone in hand, looking out the back kitchen window, it was an idyllic moment—twilight approached, bringing with it the cries of the wild parrots among the palm trees in the field beyond their property. The late smell of orange blossoms that never seemed to leave the area, whether winter, fall, or spring. They had chosen Redlands as home because it seemed so separate from the rest of the area—it had avocado trees along its hillsides, and city orange groves throughout its park system. In the summers, there was local theater, and shows at the Redlands Bowls that the kids loved as they grew up. The house itself was an old one-story L-shaped adobe that was one of the original ranch houses of what had once been miles of orange orchards. It came complete with a beautiful Spanish-style courtyard filled with bird-of-paradise, bougainvillea, and even a plum tree by its far, low wall.

And yet, the few times his job intruded—a call home, a vacation interrupted, a midnight emergency—he felt less safe. Less safe for his wife, Carly, and their two children, Mark and Teresa.

He felt that the world itself was unstable, and that something—or someone—lurked in shadows.

He felt as if the bad guys who were out there—the ones who made him sometimes wonder whether there was a God at all, given the way the human mind could create its own monsters—had stepped into the kitchen with him. At the glass table, right there, looking out on the backyard. And now he was thinking now about murder, instead of the steak he had just finished marinating for the barbeque.

He glanced across the room to his wife, chopping onions near the sink. Her hands were a blur of movement; the smell of sweet onions in the air. From the open window, he heard the bickering of scrubjays and mockingbirds at the birdfeeder in the yard. It was an ordinary day. He knew from experience it was the ordinary days that bit you in the ass and held on.

Carly grinned. "What's up?"

"The son of one of Darden's former patients is back at Darden."

"Second-generation sociopath," Carly said, a bitter edge to her voice. "Come on, I'm joking. Who was the father?"

"Mother. Mary Chilmark. Bloody Mary. That's what they called her in the press. You remember the murders?"

"Was she one of the Manson girls or something?"

"Nothing that infamous. She was a nurse who murdered a couple of patients. I can't remember the particulars. I just remember hearing some things about her. She left before I got there."

"So Jane's bringing you back into something," Carly said, and it struck Trey that she said this almost as if she meant something illicit between the two of them. "I'm glad you've got this work, but I just wish sometimes you could do the nine to five and that'd be it."

"I'm being asked to consult. That's all."

"How's that different?"

"It's with the police. And apparently against Hannafin's wishes. But in this case they're going around her. They want me to handle the intake interview."

2

What had happened to Trey over the past months had shocked him. He had been sure after the incident with the Red Angel killer that he'd be demoted, fired, or worse, hidden. But the opposite had occurred. Officer Jane Laymon and the San Pascal County Sheriff's office lobbied the state on his behalf, and a promotion had booted him up the ranks. He had already consulted on a case in Riverside in the spring, and though there were administrators at Darden State who would've liked to get rid of him because of the ensuing scandal and lawsuit after the murder of a psychiatrist, he was exonerated of all blame, and wonder of wonders—at least to Trey—actually had been asked to give monthly talks to the psychiatric community on the criminally insane mind. His new title: Psychiatric Special Project Director. The title had come with a slight bump in salary, annoyance from some of the psychiatrists on staff, and the added bonus of being called into the field when a patient of the Darden State Hospital for Criminal Justice escaped or when a potential future patient had been caught and needed what was called a "special circumstance intake" at the forensics hospital pending trial.

In the intervening months, he'd been prepping for further study by going nights to the University of Riverside, hoping to complete a master's degree in psychology within four or five years. Even Carly had conceded that the changes that came about from his few encounters with the more lively patient-inmates at Darden State had ended up being good for him and for the future life they envisioned. "You're passionate about this," she said. "I know. I have to step back sometimes. Sometimes, what goes on there is too much for me. But I know this is your path. I've seen you change these past few years, for the better. I know it's been rough. You've gone through things that I don't think I'd be able to handle more than once in a lifetime."

Then she kissed him softly on the nose and whispered, "I married a guy who likes working with psychotic killers."

"It's not that," he said. But he could not say why he loved his work so much. He couldn't express why the human mind in all its aberrations fascinated him. Why he sought to understand the sociopath, or the sexual sadist, or the one who killed simply for pleasure. It was the predator of humankind that drew him to his work, time and again. There had been—for the first fifteen years—the simple routine of the job. The lack of knowledge of opportunity elsewhere. The interest in working within the state of California, in mental health, and a complete admiration for the psychiatric profession.

But after his experiences of the past few years, he was more involved than he ever thought he'd be. He cared about the victims, but he also cared about the rehabilitation of those who committed some of the most heinous crimes.

And yet, something about his work scared him,

too. If he thought too much about it, it nearly paralyzed him.

That same fear led him to want to know more, to study further, to keep returning to the triple-fenced, guarded buildings of the forensics hospital known as the Darden State Hospital for Criminal Justice, which had once been known as the Darden State Hospital for the Criminally Insane.

In bed that night, he and his wife snuggled and talked about things other than their jobs. They made love when the snuggling turned to an awakening passion, which at forty, he welcomed. It made him feel less weary of things, and reminded him of when he and Carly had been younger and probably more passionate about each other than they were about work and the kids. When they were done, she whispered in his ear, "I have some news, sweetheart."

But he had begun drifting off to sleep—by then it was after midnight and he had a big day of meetings and talks and intake with Bloody Mary Chilmark's nineteen-year-old son—so he missed what she said.

But as soon as he woke up, it was in his head. He knew exactly what she'd said as he had gone off into dreams.

Five-fifteen A.M., time for his morning jog, but instead, he put his arms around her and said, "We're having another kid?"

"Takes you a good eight hours of sleep to get it?"

"I think I was asleep when you said it. I thought it was a dream."

"Well, it's real. I thought maybe it wasn't. But it is."

"Wow."

"You're a little more enthused than I am," she said, drawing away, crossing her arms in front of her, looking up at the ceiling. "I'm almost forty. I didn't really want this to happen."

"Surprise," he whispered, and moved over to kiss her on the forehead.

3

That morning in the courtyard in back, Trey and Carly sat in wood-slat chairs, up in the hills, looking down on the bowl of the valley with the great San Bernardino mountains in the distance, and the pitch black of roiling smoke somewhere along the range of foothills. A dazzling sunrise nestled between the yellow and pink of sky and the darkness of the hills. Peaceful. Calm. All harm was at a distance; Trey liked it that way.

Six A.M. was for Trey Campbell and his family. Before work. Before the all-consuming time spent at Darden State on Ward D. Quiet time for him and his wife out on the patio, looking down on the beautiful valley below.

Even with some fire up in the mountains blackening their view.

"The Santa Anas," Trey said. "Like clockwork."

"They're a little early," his wife said. "I thought they contained the fires."

"I think that means they let them run out of control."

He and Carly sat out along the brick walk of the small courtyard of their adobe house, which had a near-perfect view of the distant fire. The beginning of October was slightly early for the fires, but the Santa Ana winds had their own season.

"I hope it doesn't make it over here."

"It won't."

"It almost did. Last year."

"Didn't jump the freeway." He took a sip of coffee, then reached over to pick up the soy creamer. Poured a bit more in. A bit more and it was perfect. He closed his eyes, forgetting the distant fires that were the bane of the dry California summer and fall. Images of Mark as a baby, rolling around on the floor, making his "dit-do" noise and blowing spit bubbles. Teresa, with her pout and the way she grasped his finger with all her might. *Babies.* Trey opened his eyes to gaze at her. "I can't believe it."

"I know. I'm too old."

"You are not. Aunt Kelly had her first one at thirty-nine. My cousin had her fifth kid older than you."

"Not much older. Aren't you scared?"

"No way. I'm thrilled," he said. "I definitely think we should name the kid Surprise."

"Let's not tell the kids yet," Carly said.

He nodded. "Sure."

"We can always change our minds. If we want."

He let the comment sit. Everything was too new, even to Carly. He had to let it go for now. With each child they'd had, she had been skittish at first about having them. She weighed all the pros and cons, and she eventually would come out on the side of "pro." She always did. She had told him when Mark was a baby that she wished she could always keep him a baby because she loved looking at babies all the time, and he had told her that when Mark grew up and went to college, she better not still be babying him.

But even then, the pregnancy with Mark had been rough. He also remembered the birth, and how labor had to be induced, and how he spent thirty-seven hours convinced that the worst would happen. He didn't want to go through that again.

4

After they got the kids up and the showers began going and Trey went to put cereal in the bowls, he began thinking about the future, about the new baby that would enter their lives, about the disruptions it would cause, maternity leave, paternity leave, and remembering all of what they'd gone through with Mark and Teresa, so many years ago that seemed like the day before yesterday.

When his son came out of the bathroom near the den, a big towel wrapped around him, dripping all over the floor, having left the shower running and possibly overflowing on the tile of the bathroom floor, the last thing on Trey's mind was the nineteen-year-old killer he'd be interviewing within two and a half hours.

CHAPTER FIVE

1

In San Pascal, California, out along a boulevard that had yellow stucco apartments on either side of the road dawn was long past; morning had set in. Somewhere a car alarm went off, and that was enough to wrench Jane Laymon right out of her soon-forgotten dream. Jane woke up late—she'd been up 'til two A.M. going over the Flock murder case with her colleagues—and Danny, her boyfriend, had just come back into the bedroom after showering. "You always look better naked than dressed," she said, grinning. She shot a glance over at the clock-radio by the bed. Nearly eight. She normally leapt out of bed around five for an hour of running before she headed off for work.

As a joke, Danny began posing, flexing his muscles, and she had to admit that his regular workouts were paying off for him. "Dance for me," she said.

"I could put on my uniform and strip, but I draw the line at dancing," he laughed, and nearly leapt on

41

the bed. He crawled up to her, drawing the sheet back. "You slept in your clothes?"

"Gross, I know," she said. "I was too tired to take 'em off. I got my pants off, though."

"Poor overworked baby," he said, kissing her hand. Then he sat up, straddling her waist. He leaned over and began unbuttoning her shirt. "I'll help you get ready for the day."

"You are always way too much into morning sex," she said.

"Morning, afternoon, evening, late-night." He grinned. "But since somebody was out working hard all night, I think that somebody deserves a little special attention."

"Okay," she sighed, and then grinned right back at him. She lay back while he undressed her. His hands were cool against her warm skin. He kissed her nose and then her neck, and as he drew her shirt open, he kissed her throat, and then her breasts as he cupped them in his hands.

"Let's take the day off," he whispered. "Just you and me and maybe a trip to the Laguna."

"I wish," she murmured.

"You've been under a lot of stress," he said.

"You're a dirty boy."

"I know. And you like dirty boys," he said, looking up at her from her stomach, where he had begun kissing all around her navel.

As he slipped her panties off, she let the pleasure take her over. *Not a bad way to wake up on a lousy day,* she thought.

Afterward, after a shower where he got in with her

and shampooed her hair, which always drove her nuts in just the right way, she dressed in fresh clothes and switched on the TV. "No five-mile run today?"

"I told you, stress, stress, and more stress."

"A jog might help. I'll go with you."

"I can't face it. Plus, I mean, I don't want to take yet another shower."

"Want to talk about it?"

"No."

"Aw, come on. I love hearing about all the murders."

"It'll drive you nuts."

"No it won't."

"It always does."

"I promise."

"Okay. Okay. A nineteen-year-old is in custody. We're keeping him at Darden for now. He hasn't yet been formally accused, but we're keeping him there for a couple of days."

"He's insane?"

"Seems to be. And his mother also is one of the killers. She's still on the loose."

"Who'd they kill?"

"A couple up in the Heights."

"You gonna be okay?"

She leaned into the cradle of his arm. "Yeah. I think so."

"Promise me something. Promise me you won't do what you did last time. You won't go into anything unprepared."

"I was as prepared as anyone could be."

"It scares me sometimes. This world you deal with. Murderers."

"Most of them aren't dangerous to anyone but their intended victims."

"If this guy's at Darden, he's like the Red Angel. Or that other creep. The one who . . ." He didn't finish the thought, but she had to block out the memory of how she'd lost one of her eyes.

"Well, at least we know who he is. We know who his mother is. They may be monstrous, but they don't have magic abilities."

"I know. But I want you to promise me. You'll be okay. You'll be prepared."

"Scout's honor," she said, and gave him a kiss while they watched a morning talk show where the subject of murder wasn't mentioned at all.

2

At the San Pascal Sheriff's Office that day, Jane was getting her third cup of stale coffee when Tryon, who had begun working closely with the San Pascal police department on homicides, came toward her. "I've been looking for you all morning."

"Sorry. Slept in. Need those eight hours sometimes."

"There's another body," he said. "I want you to run over to the morgue and meet up with Dahl. He's there now. And there's some trailer park to get out to. And don't be late like this. Throws everything off. Davis and March already have the techs out at the trailer, so at least it'll be kept clean."

"Will do," she said. "Where's the trailer park?"

"Over in Caldwell, up on Sunset Ridge," Tryon said, and then shook his head. "We've got to catch that woman today, damn it. It's already on the news, and we're getting crank calls about seeing Bloody Mary everywhere. I don't have enough officers as it is to track 'em all down."

CHAPTER SIX

The guy was drunk and it wasn't yet seven in the morning. The bars out on Main Street didn't close sometimes until three, even though legally they had to be shut down sooner. But the one called the Silver Coyote usually had an after-hours poker game going, and he came stumbling out the backdoor sometime after six A.M., the winner for the night with a good three hundred bucks in his pocket and the need to pee real bad. His name was Nick Spitzer, he was forty-four, and Mary Chilmark had met him once or twice in her work. She was sure he'd remember her.

Sure that he'd help her.

She hadn't slept well that night, not without her son. She knew his car—a 1984 Cadillac that had gone to hell in the years Spitzer had been driving it—and it had bumper stickers plastering the back bumper that said "Sometimes I Wake Up Grumpy, Other Times I Let Her Sleep," and "There's Too Much Blood In My Alcohol System," as well as the classic, "I Got A Gun For My Wife, Best Trade I Ever Did."

It was unlocked when she found it, so she crawled inside and slept much of the night in the backseat. She only awoke when she heard Spitzer's drunken calls to his friends as they left the bar, and then his fumbling with his keys before realizing the doors were unlocked.

When he slid into the front seat, he saw her in the rear view mirror and said, "Well, looks like somebody's lucky day. Hello, baby, long time no see."

PART TWO

PART TWO

CHAPTER SEVEN

1

Caldwell, California: small, a dust bowl of a town, a landscape full of ridges and foothills and canyons, and the kinds of houses that looked as if they were meant to fall apart twenty years after they'd been built. The most noticeable landmark—one that had been there for more than a century—was the hospital.

The triple fence with razor wire; the small sensor detectors at key points along the fences; and the guard booths at every entrance and exit—all made the series of buildings look as if they were a prison. Yet the grounds looked well tended, no guard towers were in evidence, and cars drove fairly freely in and out of the main driveway. There were a few palm trees around the buildings; brief streets connected the long main building to the administration offices; the look of a corporate park built in a style that had all but vanished thirty years before.

Darden State Hospital for Criminal Justice was

nearly a town unto itself, and recently it had known prosperous times as its criminal population blossomed. Those patients who earned, bought, or otherwise obtained the insanity defense in their murder trials had worked its vegetable gardens and the great greenhouse where beautiful orchids had been grown. They had put together a Crafts and Decorative Arts workshop that produced hanging baskets and wrought-ironwork for the home that had sold well in shops in Southern California; and they had created job skills within the hospital itself, bringing a sense of pride to the patients.

However, a group called Rights Advocacy of the Penal Institutions of San Pascal County had determined that this work was enforced labor, and had lobbied to have it stopped. This particular advocacy group seemed to have a good motive on the surface, but, digging down through its layers, you'd find that the group was funded by a handful of multimillionaire land developers who wanted state money diverted from the hospital toward their own interests. Still, their lobbying efforts had a chilling effect on Darden State. The work was stopped. The gardens were left untended, the crafts workshops, the job skills—all of it stopped because the inmates were hospital patients after all, and putting them to work in some capacity was evil.

The results of this fine humanitarian effort on the part of the developers group was that within six months of the pressure on Darden to change its approach to patient care, the medications the patients were on had to be increased, the patients became more lethargic and well aware of their status as liabilities of the state, and, because the hospital itself could not increase its own funding by selling the works of its inmates, many of the guards had to be let go, despite an increase in violent attacks on hospital staff.

In the nineteenth century, Darden was simply one of the many state asylums "for the insane and inebriate," and had looked like a gothic castle. In that castle, beneath the administrative offices, sat a true dungeon that held the many so-called "night cages" that had housed the insane, the sociopaths, the tubercular, the alcoholic, the addicted, and now and then, the menopausal. If a child were irrationally violent, he might end up in the underground children's ward. If a family's daughter did not exhibit traditional feminine traits, she might be institutionalized and given what was called, in the early twentieth century, "bath therapy."

In the 1950s, the castle had been torn down and a new row of boxes had been erected, and by 1982, the current look of Darden State had emerged. It looked more like a military base than a hospital, with guard booths along its avenues that connected the wards to the administration's offices to the row of bungalows where some staff chose to live rent free, within the fenced acreage.

There were other hospitals like Darden State in California, including nearby Patton State, but none carried the level of criminal that Darden did, since it took in the killers that the other state hospitals did not handle well.

But no matter how orderly and clean the aboveground area of the hospital seemed, beneath it, the night cages still existed, and though they had not been in use for more than seventy years, it was as if, buried beneath the new, the dark ages of psychiatric treatment still waited patiently for someone to creep down and switch on the light.

Three things caused some disturbance at the Darden State Hospital for Criminal Justice the summer and fall of 2004:

The high voltage system that ran through the wards, generally above the ceilings, was taken down into the underground—into the warren of corridors and tunnels that were no longer used beneath the hospital itself. It became a two million-dollar project that had caused patients to have a disruptive season, which was no help to the staff who cared for them. The ceilings had been ripped open; work crews came through, which required more lockdown time than normal; and the sounds of the work below—scraping, hammering, and the general thumps and metal clanks below the patients rooms on the first floor led to the widespread belief that ghosts were beneath the hospital.

This was not helped by news that a graveyard was found in one of these underground tunnels, and the bones—from the patients of the late 1800s to the early 1900s—were relocated to a cemetery eight miles away.

Somewhere in all this, a news reporter with a name that seemed as fake as his hair color—Lance Victor—had decided to do a three-part documentary on the scandals, the terrors, and the take-downs of what he called "the world of the criminally insane psychopath at the murder's hotel—Darden State, in Caldwell, California."

Memo from Shelly Olsen, Executive Director, Darden State

TO ALL DARDEN STAFF:

As many of you know, a television station out of Los Angeles has been working on a three-part documentary about the Darden State Hospital, specifically recalling last year's escape of Michael Scoleri and the murder of one of our psychiatrists, as well as other unfortunate incidents here that have gained some unwanted publicity, in local media as well as national, in the past decade or so. The recent relocation of the graves from the early twentieth century have obviously focused interest here. We must come to expect that some of our community will be maligned, misrepresented, and shown in a less-than-favorable light, and realistically, none of us will be able to respond per Article 99.8 of the Media Contact handbook.

Given that the cameras continue to come into our workplace, my best suggestion is for each employee simply to do his or her finest job, speak only when a supervisor is present, or defer to your Ward supervisor. The state of California has given the television crew an open window into our day-to-day operations, and we need to accommodate this change in routine as we would any other.

I ask you to join me, your new director, in resolving to continue with the excellence and diligence and care for which Darden State is known. One last note that I wish were unnecessary: when referring to Darden on-camera, please do so as the Darden State Hospital for Criminal Justice. We have not referred to our hospital as "for the criminally insane" since the early 1980s, and we feel it casts an unfortunate light on our work here.

We have nothing to hide here, and there is no need to cover up anything in the past. There may be disciplinary measures taken should any junior staff members take it upon themselves to speak directly with the reporter or his crew.

3

Lance Victor, the television reporter, held the microphone up to Trey Campbell just as he entered the security checkpoint in the main entrance at Darden State. "Mr. Campbell, what do you think of the murder of the Flock family by Bloody Mary and her son?"

CHAPTER EIGHT

Trey held back his reaction as he looked first to the reporter and then to the cameraman. He glanced over at one of the nurses, then to the guard who stood next to him. "I'm being ambushed again?"

In front of him stood Lance Victor, who was six foot, blond, broad shouldered, and as plastic as a pretty boy of thirty could be. Lance had won Emmys for his news coverage, had been named one of the sexiest bachelors in *Los Angeles Magazine* ten years earlier and still tried to cling to the title. He had a look in his eyes that reminded Trey of one of the new patients when they arrived at Darden, before the meds kicked in.

The cameraman behind him had kept the lens on Trey, and someone nearby had a blinding light that seemed to have laser-perfect accuracy for just Trey's face.

Trey squinted into the light. "Look, we can talk about procedure and technique like we did last week, but you're not going to help anybody—least of all the victims' families—by dredging this one up today. Not this one. Go bother the police."

"The people want to know the truth," the reporter said in an incredible imitation of a sincere tone. "We know he's here. We saw the transport. This is an important aspect of this series we're filming. Why, without an arraignment, are they putting a killer in Darden State?"

"Listen to yourself," Trey said. "You believe your own bullshit?"

A guard nearby chuckled, "Get that clown outta here."

The camera came off the cameraman's shoulders; the light shut off. The cameraman said, "Come on, Lance, let's give it a rest."

The reporter gave a sharp glance to his colleague. "I just wanted a reaction," Lance Victor said, returning his attention to Trey. "It's a story. A good one."

"You want an interview with me, you schedule. No more ambushes. Understood?" Trey said. The reporter had caught him—and at least a half dozen psych techs—off guard to try to get a so-called "candid" moment too many times over the past few weeks. Often such moments took place right when a patient was going for someone's eyes, or when a violent fight had broken out and three techs had to go in and calm the patients involved, subdue them so they would not hurt themselves, get them in restraints, and still make sure they didn't get their balls ripped off in the process. The cameraman and the reporter were there to expose any little crack in the hospital, and Trey knew too well that most of the big cracks were in the administration, not among the staffs of Wards A through D.

"I want in on Program 28," Lance said.

"No way in hell."

"If you care so much about these people, Trey, you'll get me in there."

"I can't risk your life and mine just for your show," Trey said. "If you had seen what some of these guys in 28 did, you wouldn't want to do it. You're going to have to make a special arrangement with the governor if you want to get in there."

"I have people working on it," Lance said. "I believe in Program 28, Trey. I've read up on it. I know they're the most violent, sadistic patients here. I know their crimes. I can list their names for you. If you can help me get inside there, I'll have my story, and I'll make you and your co-workers look like gold. I promise."

Trey calmed down a little. "Look, for some reason, Lance, you just get my hackles up. I apologize for the reaction. I know that what you want to do is a good thing. The more the public knows about Darden, the better off everyone is. But my understanding is there's already a stack of patient refusal and authorization papers in administration that have to be processed simply because you haven't done your follow through. We're here for the patients, for the state, and so that people like you on the outside don't have to worry about these patients on the inside. We're dealing with daily stressful situations here that are not meant for anyone's entertainment."

"Why can't I bring the camera to Program 28?"

"You know why. It's for the most far-gone sadistic of the sociopathic psychopaths," Trey said. "That's not the psych term you or the state want me to say. But there you have it. And above all that, they're human beings who deserve their privacy, even here. They deserve to get treatment within their hospitalization, period."

"You mean 'incarceration,'" Lance said. "I think those people are animals. Monsters. I know what they've done to innocent victims on the outside. I've read the files. Do you think it's right that they get to hide inside here? That they get millions from the state thrown at them to keep them safe and alive?"

Trey hated the reporter for putting it that way, but something within him understood it. Sometimes, no matter how he cared for the patients, there were a handful of them that he wasn't sure deserved to live. And he hated having those thoughts. He felt that to be good at his work, he had to put that kind of mindset aside and focus on the good that could be created at Darden. He had to believe that if the psychiatric community kept studying and seeking to understand how the human mind went to the extremes it did, that something good and powerful for the betterment of life would emerge.

But many days—and nights—Trey felt exactly like the reporter.

Some people don't deserve to live.

And he knew that very thought was not far from the minds of those extreme killers themselves.

"You have got to understand that your wanting a story does not supersede privacy issues and psychiatric considerations. Only the highest clearance would get you in there, and as far as I can tell, that's the one place you're not allowed."

"Campbell, look, man to man," Lance said. "I just . . . I want to show the world what you do here. How you and the psych techs and psychologists are . . . well, heroes of sorts. The truth of all this."

Trey wasn't sure whether to laugh or cry. *What bullshit.* "Show them whatever truth you decide on. But don't expect me to spoon-feed it to you. If you want to get clearances and permission, you know where Olsen's office is, and you know where Sacramento is if you need more than that. Now, I've got work to do."

Lance Victor sighed, and for just a split second Trey felt a twinge of sympathy for the guy. *Just doing his job.* Trey had even watched Lance's reportage on the big earthquake a few years back, and had felt the guy was pretty good. He just hadn't known how in-your-face he got until the camera came into Darden.

"I just want something exciting to happen here," Lance said.

"I know, it's pretty boring," Trey said. "It's not like the snake pit you wanted."

"Hey, you got a take-down last week," a guard at the desk said. "How much more excitement you want? You wanna riot, stick around. Maybe it'll be your lucky day."

"Yeah," Lance Victor said, grinning with perfectly capped, brilliantly white teeth. "I want a riot."

CHAPTER NINE

1

Trey nodded to the guards at the entrance to Ward A—
I.D. badge out, he passed through. The halls of A were
decorated with drawings and paintings done by the
patients. These were the least dangerous patients at
Darden—some of them had attempted suicide and
perhaps hurt someone else, but often it had been
unintentional. Still, the state put them here rather than
in a regular psych hospital, and there was good reason
for some of them. A few psychopaths had open-door
policies here, as well, for they weren't dangerous to
any but their original victims; some were in their sev-
enties and eighties, and had been at Darden State for
more than thirty years. Ward A was low security,
where the patients could mingle with the staff, have
small birthday celebrations. During visiting days, family and friends might come through and spend time
with them. All in all, it fairly closely resembled a hos-

pital ward at nearly any other hospital, but in this one, the residents tended to be fairly long-term.

He passed through the checkpoint at Ward C and nodded to Rita Paulsen, who was standing with two psych techs. When she saw him, she walked over and mentioned the TV reporter gunning for him. "I already got gunned," he chuckled, and then he stopped by the refreshment lounge and popped a dollar in a machine to get a can of apple juice.

When he reached Ward D, Pete Atkins, a Correctional Officer whose post usually was at the entryway to Program 28, stood there, waiting for him.

2

Atkins was a beefy, muscular guy. He looked the way Trey figured most people on the outside thought of the guards: commanding, imposing, and even a little threatening. He looked like he could crush skulls in his hands and still feel good about himself.

"We're keeping Chilmark in 28," Atkins told Trey when he'd gotten past security at Ward D. "We had a minor incident earlier."

They both walked swiftly down the hallway. Now and then Trey glanced in the windows of the therapy rooms, to see what groups were already in session.

"How's Victor know about the Chilmark kid being here?"

"He's in the news biz. They know," Atkins said, walking slightly ahead of Trey.

"I was sick of seeing that guy a month and a half ago," Trey said. "He's like the bogeyman, popping up when you least expect him. I don't want him to even know where Chilmark is. I wish Lance Victor would just go back to L.A."

"Hannafin keeps him close," Atkins said, and then smirked. "She probably wants a new book deal, so she keeps the publicity going around her."

"Where is she anyway? She should be here."

"Running late. Start without her. That's what she said."

Trey walked swiftly down the corridor, stopping by his office briefly to pick up the clipboard that had the material from Hannafin and from the police. "Was he given meds?"

"As per Dr. Hannafin, no."

"Good. Was he hurt in the take-down?"

"Not visibly. But it took six of us. I want you to know that, Trey. He's like a mountain lion when he's not in restraints."

"Did he get anybody?"

"Minor knee injury to Feldman. Other than that, once we had him on the floor, he calmed down. He took the restraints fine. In fact, he practically started purring when the jacket went on."

"I want the restraints off, if possible."

"Not yet, Trey," Atkins said. "He has another hour in them. Then he can get out. That's per Hannafin herself. She wants a two-hour minimum restraint period if a patient doesn't yet have meds, until all intake and assessment is complete. It's purely a safety measure. For the patient."

At the entryway to what the staff called the "silver wing" of Darden State, Trey showed his security badge, a formality that had to be observed in order to get through the double doors into Program 28. He didn't bother glancing in the other rooms that he passed, but kept moving down to the very last room where the temporary patient had been housed.

Program 28 was still relatively new, and funds for it had begun wavering already. It had cost a fortune to equip, and had been set up to take on all the Sexually Violent Offenders divided into a few classes of human predator. They tended to be the patients no other hospital wanted, and they required additional expense to house. But the staff psychiatrists nearly begged the board to okay the funds for the program, and it was their little golden egg—both prestige and money flowed to the department with Program 28. It was considered the worst of the worst, in terms of killers, and Trey wasn't even sure that Doc Chilmark belonged down in it.

The new patient was not sexually violent, but because the rooms were nearly their own isolation tanks for the patients, it served the purpose of keeping Chilmark out of the general population of Ward D.

The corridor had a blue-green metal cast to it, and shone as the overhead lights bounced off the steel doors. Thick panes of observation glass separated the patient from the staff. The rooms themselves were spare. The cot and table were secured to the floor. A sink and toilet sat in one corner of the room, and a narrow and barred window was far above the reach of any patient.

At the locked door to the patient's quarters, Trey waited for the others to arrive before unlocking and entering the room.

CHAPTER TEN

1

The room was well lit, but Trey wished there were a dimmer switch. In the white light, the killer looked like a little abused boy who was only just beginning to look like a man. Trey had already spent most of the morning going over the killer's mother's past records at Darden State, and briefly had seen some photos from the recent crime scene at the house in the foothills, faxes sent in as soon as Jane Laymon knew he'd be showing up for the intake evaluation with Chilmark.

In the photos: a woman on a bed. Dark blotches all over the mattress.

A man on a staircase, his bloody handprints all along the walls.

And this man—this boy who had just recently become a man—had done it.

With his mother.

Instruments used include a scalpel, a bonesaw, a

bone file, bandage scissors, large metal forceps, several hypodermic needles, and what looked like a medium-sized hammer with a coin-sized circular saw attached to it and a sharp point at its tip. The note by the picture: "Atrephine for trepan."

Sitting behind Trey was a psychologist named Whitfield, a young man himself, just out of his master's program, in the room to observe. Whitfield had thin wisps of prematurely thinning blond hair, and a wide face that would have seemed cherubic, except he rarely smiled. He was one of the most serious of the younger group of psychologists, and had made it known to Trey in past encounters that he did not intend to be anything other than cold and professional.

Trey leaned back in his chair and whispered, "Thanks for coming."

Whitfield remained silent.

In the doorway stood a correctional officer with a big gut and a stern look.

Trey glanced up from his clipboard, to the patient.

He marked in his notes: *Patient has ankle hobbles. In straitjacket. Appears calm.*

The patient was approximately five-foot-four, with brown hair that had not been cut in awhile, narrow shoulders, narrow hips. Not exactly a slight build, but something about him was elfin. The snapshot taken upon his arrest did not resemble him much with the exception of the faint scars on his face. He looked angry in the photo. Here, in person, he seemed calm. He was relaxed, even in restraints. He looked like a nice guy who had run a red light and somehow ended up here, but was good-humored about it.

The scars, though faint, had been from being burnt and possibly sliced, but so many years before that they'd healed over. There were likely similar scars along his arms and legs as well. Trey easily guessed the reason: Mommy. She had been torturing the kid since birth. She had probably burned him with cigarettes and matches, and possibly taken a knife to his face more than once. It amazed Trey how sometimes a child could survive and grow up in such an environment at all. It surprised him whenever they turned out to be sane.

Chilmark was no surprise. His mother had raised him to be a psychopath, probably. She had done her damnedest to make him into her own image, and had apparently succeeded.

Trey swallowed his feelings of compassion for the moment. The guy had just murdered a woman, a man, and an unborn child.

Tortured or no. Abused for years, perhaps, but it was hard for Trey to get around the images of the dead he'd seen.

Plus, Chilmark was smiling at him.

His smile was amiable. In fact, he seemed too comfortable.

In the fluorescent light, his skin was pallid. He had spent a lot of time avoiding the Southern California sun. Streaks of scars, pale, and somehow far too happy.

From where he sat, Trey wasn't sure if there was a birthmark of some kind on his neck, or if it was a tattoo. Some discoloration on the left side of his neck where it slipped down beneath the collar of the strait-jacket.

Trey had a photo of the patient's mother from the 1980s. The patient resembled her quite a bit, and also resembled—in his nose and lips and something even in his eyes—the psychiatrist who might, in fact, be the patient's father.

Trey wondered if Dr. Brainard would show up for any of the intake or evaluations related to the young man who might be his son.

2

"I want to see a priest," the patient said.

"We can arrange that. Catholic or Episcopalian?"

"Catholic."

"Mr. Chilmark," Trey began. "Do you understand why you're here?"

"Doc."

"Excuse me?"

"I've been called Doc since I was a little kid." His voice was soft but deep, and it sounded as if he'd practiced speaking in order to come up with such a smooth delivery.

Trey kept his eye on Jane Laymon's notes. Then he looked up.

The patient was handsome, troubled, muscled, looking far too innocent for someone who had just committed the atrocities that Trey had seen in those photos of the victims.

Chilmark looked like an ordinary, healthy American

youth, basically. Not completely clean cut and not terribly experienced. But that was a mask, sometimes. A mask for deeper, hidden secrets.

Certainly for this young man, the secrets were just about coming out into the light of day.

"But your name is Quentin. Quentin Chilmark."

"Everyone calls me Doc."

"Why 'Doc'?"

"Doctor Quentin Chilmark. But please. I've been Doc since I was a kid."

"Tell me about medical school."

The edges of the patient's lips curled slightly. He chuckled to himself. "Do you know about talent? Some people are born with it. Some have it thrust upon them. Some have to earn a degree to pretend they have it. Before doctors, there were healers. And those healers didn't need to go to college. They had talent. When you have it, you don't need to be taught the craft of medicine. You know it."

"You're a healer?"

"I understand the nervous system of living things. I know how to set it right. I see death sometimes. Not the way people think. It's in shadows. Shadows of those who have already passed."

"Ghosts?" Trey asked. "Are you psychic?"

"I see people who have died, yes. Sometimes. They've taught me the secrets. The healing arts. The meanings of things. They brought it out in me, this talent. Some people are born with beautiful voices. Training only ruins them. My talent is healing, and my art is medicine for the body and soul. I have my father's hands and my mother's heart."

"Do you understand why you're here?"

"Sometimes, when a doctor does something for a patient's well-being, he ends up blamed for something he didn't do."

Trey leaned back in his chair. "You're here until a trial date is set. At that point, you'll be transferred to a facility in Los Angeles County. I imagine you'll just be here a few weeks."

"I'm here because my mother once spent time here."

"Yes, your mother was here."

"She was pregnant with me then."

"Ah."

"My father was a psychiatrist. He had troubles early on. I never knew him."

Trey refrained from telling all he knew, the rumors that Dr. Brainard was Bloody Mary Chilmark's lover before she was discharged into the arms of another psychiatrist, who married her briefly before taking his own life.

Dr. Brainard had denied it in a formal inquiry, and it remained rumor. Brainard now ran the Psychiatric Board of Darden, and although he was a difficult man, Trey had never believed he'd stoop to entering into an intimate relationship with a patient. It was a popular delusion among some of the patients—that their doctor was also their lover.

Trey checked off the intake questions one by one, knowing that they'd get passed on to the psychiatrist who would handle the patient's therapy for the time he was in Darden State. He became conscious of Whitfield behind him, who was probably wondering why he wasn't asking more pointed questions at this stage.

Provoking the patient was sometimes as important as gathering specific information. Sometimes the patient said exactly what needed to be said.

In this case, Trey's directive from Jane Laymon was to try to get Chilmark to tell where his mother might be hiding.

"I'll bet you're writing fun stuff in that little clipboard of yours," Chilmark said. "I'll bet you're mentioning that I show no remorse. That I am in a state of delusional thinking."

"I'm not qualified to assess you in that way," Trey said. "This is called the preliminary intake. We do it with new patients or with those, like you, awaiting trial, who have been recommended to this facility. Do you know why you've been recommended here?"

"They want to catch her."

Trey kept his poker face. It was important not to show the slightest surprise at one of the patient's answers. "It's because of the nature of the crime committed."

"Alleged crime."

"I have photos from the crime scene. Would you like to see them?"

"No."

"Why not?"

"They're fake."

"Why not look at them to see for yourself?"

"I don't need to. I was there. We were working to help that woman."

"She was six months pregnant. But she's dead now. And her child within her. And her husband."

"Sometimes when you attempt healing, the spirit leaves the body. If you could see spirits, you'd know."

73

"Do you see spirits here? With us?"

The patient broke eye contact with Trey, and looked around the room at the others. "Not right here. Not right now. They make themselves known to me as shadows."

"At this house. Where you say you healed. What shadows were there?"

"The dead are everywhere around us," he said. "Most people are too caught up in the illusion of movement to recognize them. But some people see them."

"Healers?"

The patient nodded.

"You look uncomfortable. Would you like the restraints taken off?"

"No. I heart my straitjacket," he said.

"You like it?"

"I love it. When I was little, I had one of these. It kept me calm. More kids should be put in them," Chilmark said. "It was like warmth all around me. I loved it. I love it now. It's a blanket of love. Sometimes, if I was just tied down right, I felt completely at peace. Like I do now."

Trey scribbled a few notes. Behind him, Whitfield cleared his throat as if about to ask something, but no question came.

"You can sit down if you like. That might be more comfortable." Trey had the correctional officer get a chair and bring it in for the patient. When Chilmark sat down, he closed his eyes and whispered something.

"I'm sorry. Would you mind repeating that?"

"Yes, I mind."

"Are you thirsty?"

"No."

"I'd like to ask you more about these shadows you see."

"If you look, you'll see them, too."

"Did you see them when you tried to heal the woman?"

The patient shot a harsh look at Trey. Trey felt an unpleasant intensity in the young man's expression. "Their shadows left them. It was the healing. Their bodies were already decaying. They needed to move to the light."

"The light of heaven?"

"I can't say. I've never gone to it. My mother thinks it's heaven. I just know it's where they go."

"Does your mother see them, too?"

"No. But she knows I do."

"Where is she right now?"

"Everywhere. She is love. She is the most beautiful being on this planet. She is light itself. Light in the darkness. She is in everything. She's always watching."

"Even now?"

"Right now. She's watching. When I was a boy, she could go through these doors in my mind and see what I was thinking. She still can. That's her talent. Mine is for healing."

"Is she nearby? Watching you now?"

He grinned, shaking his head. "She told me wonderful things about this place. She told me that there were shadows of death along the corridors. She told me that no one who had entered this place ever really left. It seems fitting that I'm here."

"How so?"

"I was conceived here. It's my womb," he said. "Inside my mother, I felt the howl of Darden State."

"You were born in 1985. After your mother's release."

"I was here, inside her, for four months. It's like coming home," he said. "I belong here. It called to me. Home at last. She told me about it. She told me that it wasn't as bad as you'd think. She's right. It's not. I like it here. I could stay here a long, long time."

Trey cleared his throat. "Tell me about her," he said.

"She's pure love," Doc Chilmark said. "She's like fire. She's that pure."

CHAPTER ELEVEN

1

Dr. Susan Hannafin waited for him in the hallway outside. She was dressed smartly in a tailored suit with a skirt that showed off her legs. She wore the white jacket required of all psychiatrists when on the Ward, but even with that, she looked better than she had a right to look. She had no trouble confirming her status as the resident celebrity psychiatrist—with her makeup, the neatly trimmed bangs, and her clothes, she was nearly always camera-ready. She was also the only black female psychiatrist in residence at Darden, and that added something to her celebrity, as well. Plus, there was the book she'd written. Truth was, Trey felt a little intimidated by her and a bit dazzled by her presence.

"How'd it go?" she asked.

"Good. So far. Want my notes?" Trey said, passing them to her.

She glanced at them briefly and put the clipboard

back in his hands. "Let's get those typed up. I'm going to spend part of today and then I hope most of the morning tomorrow with Chilmark. I don't want him to be alone too much. I think there's some good work to be done with him—even if he only ends up staying here a month or two before the county starts the case up."

"He might be here longer."

"That's assumed," she said. "We can't keep him in 28 too long, but maybe we can find a place for him in D. What's your arrangement with the investigation?"

"Basic consult. No spying, don't worry." He said this last bit as a slight joke, but he could tell that it didn't go over well by the rather blank expression on Hannafin's face.

"The patient's rights are a bit void at this point," she said, and then when Whitfield came from the room, she drew him over and they began what Trey often characterized as a "whisper-conference," made to make him remember that his position at Darden was still lower than a staff psychologist. After a few moments of whispering, Hannafin came back over to Trey, put her arm on his elbow and said, "You've done great. We'll take over from here. If one of the detectives needs to talk to him, let's suggest either an early evening or early morning meeting."

"Dr. Hannafin," he said. "Look. I know you aren't happy, having me assigned to this. I'll do my best to serve your needs here. And I promise to stay out of your way the rest of the time."

Hannafin glanced at Whitfield, then back to Trey. "I'm not unhappy that you're working on this with me, Trey. What gave you that idea?"

"Well, I know that you prefer to keep this—"

"You're good at what you do. I'm not thrilled that your consult is with a homicide investigation, but I understand how the needs of Darden and the needs of the community at large are sometimes at variance. I have no problems with this arrangement. I have seven patients to see today, and if you can work up your evaluation, get it on my desk this afternoon, believe me, my job just got easier. I appreciate it. I'm glad you're on this, frankly."

And then she took off down the corridor again before he could say anything more. Whitfield shot him an odd glance as if to say, *Don't you feel stupid?*

2

"Call Father Joe for Chilmark," Trey told Jim Anderson after the intake, once he'd gotten back to his office. Jim was not only one of Trey's best old friends—at Darden just about as long as Trey had been—he was the only one who got his jokes, his asides, understood the inside and out of irony, and had been with Trey in more take-downs of wild patients than anyone else in the hospital. Jim was a big linebacker of a guy, but he still had the face of a kid with his fingers in the cookie jar. If Anderson had stayed at the job, working now directly with Trey on Ward D and Program 28, Trey felt he probably would've ended up in restraints himself.

"You think we'll get a confession?" Jim asked. He took the chair opposite Trey's desk, leaning back in it, checking his pager.

"I don't give a damn. That'll be Laymon's issue. He

wants to talk to a priest, let's get a priest in to him. I feel bad for this guy."

"A guy who just ripped a baby out of a woman's body?" Jim asked, even while he clicked through his pager messages.

"That kid was abused. In ways you and I probably have trouble imagining. Darden State made a mistake twenty years ago by releasing his mother. Someone made a mistake by impregnating her. That boy is paying for the mistake, and I'm guessing he's been paying his whole life. He thinks a straitjacket is comforting. Like a teddy bear."

"I don't buy it," Anderson said. "A lot of kids get abused who don't do what he did."

"Maybe they didn't get abused in quite that way."

"What way?"

"He was raised to be the perfect lover to his mother. Who knows how long that's gone on. Who knows what toll it's taken on him."

Anderson winced. "Ew, incest. Yeesh. Can't imagine. You think that's it?"

"Yep. And somewhere in there, he was physically abused to the breaking point. He thinks he's a doctor because she made him fix himself. Did you see his arm? It was slightly askew at the elbow. I didn't notice 'til the jacket came off. She's broken his bones. Maybe years ago. I'm guessing he had to set them himself. I'm guessing he had to heal his own body when he was a little boy. He had to be his own doctor."

"Did you see Whitfield? Hear no evil, see no evil," Jim said, putting his hands over his ears. "He sat there like a bump on a log and you know he's going to somehow make the intake all about him. He always does."

"He's definitely got issues with me working with Hannafin. But she surprised me. I thought she wanted me completely off this case, but she seemed great about it."

"Yeah, I can never tell with her," Jim said. "Sometimes she's a ball-buster and sometimes she's pretty reasonable. I like strong women like that. It's kind of cool."

Trey drew out the notebook computer from the side table at his desk and opened it up.

"Want me to leave?"

"No. Just gonna type up some of my impressions. You on break?"

"Taking a breather. I have to get down to 28 and check on Ivory and Mandolar. Atkins and Freeman told me something's up down there, and Paulsen doesn't want to deliver any meals if she can help it unless at least three of us are there to help out." He glanced at his watch. "I figure I have ten minutes to kill. I call it my coffee break."

They sat around, Trey typing in his evaluation, and Jim shooting the breeze about stuff he was up to out in the world—what was up at home, how he wanted to go deep sea fishing in a couple of weeks out at Point Mugu. Paula Stewart, a psych tech on Ward D, came by the office and told him that someone had escaped into the underground.

"Who?" Trey asked.

"Fallon," she said. "Somehow he got through the canteen."

"Rob Fallon? Christ. Can anyone else handle this?"

"Hannafin requested you for it."

"And I shall hop to it," Trey said. "This is what, the third time?"

"Fourth. You forgot Candler. She got in there, too. Back in July," Paula said. "Didn't get beyond the fifth step down, though."

"Oh yeah. Do those guys hauling the wires ever lock the door behind them? Do they not understand where they're working?" Trey asked, shaking his head as if already knowing the answer. "Okay, well, thanks, Paula. I don't get this place sometime. Tight as hell security at the gate, but inside . . ."

"It's a free for all, sure," she said. "You want me to help?" But even as she asked this, he could tell by her tone that she had other things to get back to on Ward D. She was one of the best, and often had been run ragged by the psychologists who liked to assign everything to her because of her volunteerism.

"No, it's okay. I'll go down there with Jim," Trey said, glancing over at Jim, who had a big smile plastered on his face. "I appreciate the offer. Thanks."

"Robby'll be easy enough to nab," Jim said. "Like stealing candy from a baby."

"Reminds me," Trey said. "All morning I forgot to tell you—we're having another rugrat in the Campbell household."

CHAPTER TWELVE

1

Trey Campbell and Jim Anderson walked down the institutional-green hallway, recently painted and still smelling of turpentine; the groans and chattering of patients and staff somewhere nearby was a low hum as they passed by nurses with their squeaky med carts and the open-door therapy sessions.

They walked past the inmate-patients of Program 6 on Ward D. Some of the inmates looked out through the rounded double-glass windows. It always gave Trey a strange feeling whenever he saw them like this—as if *they* were observing details about the staff.

"I can't believe you're having another kid," Jim said.

"Yeah, weird, huh? Two kids already, and now we start again."

"How pregnant?"

"Six weeks."

"Hey, you should tell Mark that this one's a replacement model and he needs to scoot."

"Very funny, wiseguy. We're holding off on telling the kids. Just for a bit."

"Carly?"

"She's still in shock. Here she was, thinking she couldn't really have anymore, after all that trying about six years ago. She told me she thought she was past her expiration date."

"Aw, you guys are still a little young for that," Jim laughed. "Hell, you could probably have four more kids."

"I suspect this'll be the last one." Trey sighed. "I guess I just knew my home office would get turned into another kid's bedroom someday."

"That's what they're for," Jim said, slipping his hand across Trey's shoulder. "Three kids is perfect. You can't get good sibling rivalries going with just two kids. Plus, you know hand-me-downs. And the blue-skies take of all this is that Teresa can actually baby-sit so you won't be stuck at home every Friday night."

"I love being with the kids on Friday night, Jim. I really do. My dad had all these hobbies and problems and other things. I just like being there with the kids. I like the idea of a big family. I'm good with this. Carly's a little overwhelmed. But I can't wait. You know, though, I'm going to be old. I mean really old, when the kid's heading to college."

"You'd be old with or without another kid," Jim said. "Man, I am so happy for you both. You're lucky. And that kid's going to be damn lucky to have a daddy like you."

"Yeah," Trey said. "If I keep both my eyes intact."

"You and me both."

They walked around the workers who had to repair damage to the upper grillwork, along the fluorescent lights. A group session was going on in the Merritt Room—Trey saw Hannafin conducting. For just a second she glanced out the open door, and then said something to the attending psych tech, who got up from his chair outside the circle and went to close the door.

"I think you should name him after me," Jim said, a twinkle in his eyes. "I mean, after all, Jim's a good name. If it's a girl, name her Hulga."

"Hulga?"

"Well, or Jim. Jim can be a girl or a boy. Jim's the best name there is."

"That's true." Trey grinned. "Many good Jims. Like Jimmy Dean."

"Jimmy Cagney."

"Jimmy Cricket."

"That's Jiminy."

"Same thing. Jim Beam."

"Jimmy Durante."

"Jimmy Smits."

"Jim Thorpe," Jim said, and by the time they got to the back of the canteen, they'd gone through a good fifteen well-known Jims and had started in on famous Hulgas, which made Jim crack up because he realized there were none.

By then, they'd made it through two locked doors, which Trey carefully relocked behind them. They'd gone from the sterile halls of Darden State to the stainless steel kitchen of Ward D's canteen. The clean-up crew was scrubbing down pans and washing out the grease pits and griddles from breakfast. The industrial dishwashers steamed up Trey's glasses to the point that he had to take them off and brush them against his breast pocket every now and then.

"Fallon get in here through the pipes?" Trey looked up at the grillwork and the heating pipes that ran along the industrial green ceiling.

Jim shot him a look. "Easier than that. One of these state guys left the door open. We locked it up afterward so he couldn't get out again."

The small room they entered after the third locking and unlocking, unlike the others, was made of cinderblocks. Trey tapped the wall. "Under these are the old stones. Quarried from the foothills."

"Jesus, it stinks down here," Jim said.

"Can't believe he even knows about this place."

"When one of our boys wants a hidey-hole, you can't really stop 'em."

"You'd think the cameras would." Trey pointed up to the top corner of the room, just behind the door. A slim beige camera was mounted there, little more than a lens and a rounded hump of camera. The techs all called it the Watcher, and Trey had no better name for it. They'd installed them within the past two years. Some Watchers were larger than others because they wanted the inmates to know that someone supervised them at all times. It helped with the sociopaths, who tended to obey the rules so long as they thought someone watched them.

Some Watchers, like this one, were smaller, almost like the Internet cams Trey had seen in computer stores—barely noticeable until you gave a room the once-over. These were generally installed where fewer patients had access, and if someone breached the area—either staff or inmate—someone higher up the food chain would notice via security.

Trey reached up for the Watcher, but couldn't quite touch it. He glanced at Jim, who, much taller, had no problem grasping the camera and giving it a gentle tug.

Just as Trey had thought, the camera came out of its mount too easily.

Wires had been cut.

Then he pointed to the narrow low doorway, with the thick wooden door that seemed to him almost something out of Hansel and Gretel.

"Do you think he's down there alone?" Jim asked.

"Sure."

"How the hell would he even know about this place?"

"Staff talks. He's pretty good at being unobtrusive. With all the rewiring going on, he probably just listened to the workers over the summer."

"He's a little weasel."

"Rob Fallon's a genius," Trey said, glancing at the door. "What tools you got?"

"Basics. Tazer if necessary."

"Not necessary."

"I don't trust the little lying son-of-a-bitch."

"Trust isn't the issue. Anyone else down there? Guys working on the voltage system?"

"All of 'em got called up once they heard a patient was down there."

"Good."

Jim pulled his walkie-talkie out. Before he pushed

the button to speak, he glanced at Trey. "Just calling some C.O.s over. We might need firepower. I don't like taking chances with Fallon."

"In all the years you've known Fallon, when was the last time he hurt anyone on staff?"

"He did a number on Donna Howe."

Trey grimaced. He hated thinking about it. Howe had been killed because she had been seduced by Rob Fallon's charm. It was a problem for a good-looking sociopath—there were men and women out there who might as well have had the word "Victim" emblazoned on their foreheads. And Rob, the Adonis Murderer, had been all too willing to charm his victims into giving up their lives—or limbs—when he'd been outside Darden.

"That was Hatcher, not Fallon. Fallon may have set it up, but Hatcher did the slicing," Trey said. "Christ, maybe we should call one of the guards. Who you recommend?"

"That new guy. Floyd. He's always talking about how he wants to see what's down here," Jim said. "Now's his chance."

2

Floyd Nelson was a fifth-generation Californian. It had been his dream to be a cop in San Bernardino, but when it hadn't worked out, he'd gone into the field of corrections, first working, fresh-faced and upbeat, at Chuckawalla State Prison, maximum security. He had loved it so much that he'd had to undergo a series of psychological tests after he was caught beating an inmate within an inch of his life. Instead of getting dumped out of the system, he'd been transferred to the Darden State Hospital for Criminal Justice, and, at twenty-five, had decided to stop beating up inmates and start learning to handle them. He was tall and lanky and a little bit scrawny. His legs were too long for his body, and his uniform always looked like it didn't quite fit him. He had a happy look about him, and was quick to hum a tune while at his post over at the checkpoint between C and D. They'd cut back on correctional officers to the point that some at Darden were getting a little nervous about supervision, but Floyd had enough energy to do the job of two guards.

Trey had watched Floyd handle take-downs well enough to know that his story about getting a bad rap from his fellow prison guards might've been the main reason for his problems at Chuckawalla. Sometimes, the guards themselves could be the problem. Sometimes, the guards were heroes. It was like anything else in life—you never knew with some of them. There was good and bad in the staff; good and bad in the patients. You couldn't always separate it out. Trey had come to learn after all the years at the hospital that you just had to deal with it all.

Trey had a lot of respect for any officer who worked with criminals in the system, and had met more good ones than bad ones. He was pretty sure Floyd Nelson was one of the good ones, despite what was in his file.

Trey knew enough about personnel files to know that sometimes they didn't tell the whole truth.

Only two things annoyed the hell out of people on the floor about Floyd. First, he was always smacking gum in his mouth, and it never seemed to faze him when people complained about the noise. And second, he had a voice that came out somewhere between his nose and his eyeballs. People assumed he couldn't help it, but the shrill sound of him sometimes even upset the prisoners.

He was an odd duck.

3

Floyd Nelson arrived on the scene within minutes of the call, and although he had his club with him and his gun holstered, he said, "Eh, if it's Fallon, I'll just sweet-talk him."

"You been down there before?" Trey asked.

Nelson, looking like a Boy Scout of twenty-five who would volunteer for wrassling a mountain lion, shook his head. Smacked his gum, acting cocky. "Barely. Just looked down. It's all this stuff going on. Rewiring and shit. Didn't go far, but far enough to not like it down there."

"I've been all over it," Jim said. "Once. Back in the olden days, about nine years ago. They used to take us down here. Just to show us."

"It's like one big dungeon, that's what one of the guys told me," Floyd said, his grin spreading ear-to-ear, his hand lightly touching the edge of his holster. "Or a rat maze, I guess."

"Floyd, can I ask that you just don't chew gum when we're working together?" Jim asked. "It's like hearing a clock ticking real loud."

"I need gum. It keeps my mouth from dryin' out."

"Come on, dude. Spit it out. You can get some more when we get Fallon out of there. Please. Oh please. If I get another migraine, I'm gonna go postal," Jim said.

Floyd glanced over at Trey, who said nothing. Then he spit the gum into his hand, and then put it up behind his ear, which made Jim wince a little. "Please tell me you're not gonna chew that later on."

"My ear's clean," Floyd said.

4

"It's a series of cells, operating rooms, and administrative offices," Trey said. "Not much different from what's above. Just think of it like that. He may have squirreled himself down in one of the tunnels, and then we're a little screwed. But it's just a big basement if you think about it."

"Big frickin' basement," Jim said with a grin. "Back when lobotomies and shock treatment were the norm. And drunks got put away."

Trey nodded grimly. "The dark ages of psychiatry."

"They still do shock treatments in Mercato," Floyd said. "At least, that's what I heard."

"They may want to, but they don't," Trey said.

I hate going down here, he thought. No matter what anyone said, nobody who worked in the aboveground hospital liked going below. Most of them forgot about it. Most tried not to think about what was below their feet as they walked the corridors of Darden.

And then he drew the door back.

"I once had to go down there with two others because the pipes had some problems," Jim said.

"There are tunnels heading all over the place. Rooms so small it makes you want to run out of there fast. And I did, believe me. I found a place where there was an incinerator."

"A furnace?" Trey asked.

"An incinerator. Back in the day, when someone with tuberculosis died, they had to burn the body on the premises, by law. I hated even seeing that thing. Big old ugly metal furnace that looks like it could fit six people comfortably, and twelve if you stacked 'em. Creepy, creepy. I wish they'd just fill it with concrete and brick the whole thing over."

"How far does it go? A mile?" Floyd asked. "When I was down there it looked like it went on forever."

"The whole length and breadth of the grounds above us, pretty much. If Fallon's down there right now, he's staying put, though. Some of the wings of the underground got caved in. Like back where they found the burial area. But I don't think anyone's gone exploring down here for at least a decade. Who knows?"

"I heard somebody tried to escape under the street coming up from down here," Jim said. "But that was before my time."

He toggled a couple of switches just inside the doorway. A green-yellow light came on, and then a red one just inside the narrow corridor that awaited them.

"Gentlemen," Trey said. "Start your engines."

"Sort of exciting in a weird way," Jim said, turning back to look at the corrections officer. "Hey, Floyd, you ready for a take-down?"

And that's when they heard someone coming up behind them. Well, smelled him first. The strong cologne was smothering as it moved ahead of the man who walked rapidly toward them.

Trey glanced behind his back. Lance Victor and his cameraman were in the doorway. The camera's red light was on, and Lance looked like he had just won the lottery.

CHAPTER THIRTEEN

1

"No, no, and no," Trey said. "Floyd, escort Mr. Victor and his camera guy—what's your name?"

"Carl," the cameraman said.

"Okay, Floyd, let's get Carl and Mr. Victor back to the canteen, please."

"I just want to get a shot or two down there," Lance Victor said. His face was shiny with sweat, and his hair had matted against his scalp. "We can do it on low-light, so you won't even notice us."

"I'm sorry, sir," Floyd said. "I've got to ask you, for your own safety, to step back into the other room until we've come out of here."

"I've been in riots before," Lance said. "I've had a murderer point a gun at me when the camera was on. It's all right. I know you can handle this guy. This just would really make the series click."

"I'm sorry," Trey said.

"Look, this guy could rip your face off," Jim said,

turning grim. "I've seen him tear a man limb from limb."

"I've met this inmate," Lance said. "Robert Fallon. I doubt he could tear anyone up."

"Then you've never seen him at his best. He's in here for slicing a woman up. Well, several people, actually. Sometimes he scalps them. Nobody's here because they committed a nice neat murder," Jim said. "You ever see a staffer with one eye? Or the ones who limp a little? Attacks are the norm."

"No matter what," Trey said, "we have a responsibility to protect the patients from this kind of exploitation. Even if we took you down there, Mr. Victor, your network would never be able to run that segment. You know that. Without our explicit permission, and the permission of the state, you can't expose a patient like this. Now, go back into the canteen. Or go find one of the administrators to take you on a tour of Ward D. You can probably sit in on a group. All right?"

Lance Victor drew his cell phone out of his pocket, flicked it up, and tapped in a number. He spoke into the phone and then passed it to Trey.

Trey put it to his ear, and heard the voice of the executive director of Darden State, James Willard. "Trey, we've given him access. The state has approved this."

After he closed the phone, he tossed it back to Lance. "Stay close. Do not start interviewing anyone. Do not talk to the patient if you see him. If he comes for you, scream as loud as you can so that we hear you. If you and your camera guy decide to go off on your own, we can't guarantee your safety. Also, and listen up, there are some high-voltage wires down there, not all of them secure. My advice is, don't touch one if you see it hanging from the ceiling. And one command. Do not talk to me. Do not ask me questions. Do not stand directly behind me at any time once we're down there. Stay back at least three feet. This is for your own safety. Understood?"

Both Lance Victor and his cameraman, Carl, nodded. Carl asked, "What's it like down there?"

Floyd Nelson grinned, glancing at the others. "I've been down twice already since July. It's not all that bad. Just some old administration offices, some corridors that don't really lead anywhere anymore. Rooms, basically. Crumbling a little. Messy. But it's just like you'd expect old offices to look that haven't been used in a long time."

"It's not precisely a dungeon," Trey said. "At least not where we're going."

2

The stairway down was metal, and had been built in 1994 when the old staircase had given way after nearly a century of neglect. The steps and banister were almost ornate in structure, and shivered slightly with so many people on it. "Maintenance guys come down here more than anybody," Trey said, and turned his flashlight on as he descended the staircase. The light below grew feeble as they went down, and Trey sensed something bad there.

"Jesus," Jim said. "I wish we didn't have five people going down. It's gonna make Fallon panic."

"It'll be okay," Trey said. "We'll handle it. I'm betting that Rob wishes he hadn't run down here at all at this point."

"I heard a few other patients got down here," Lance said, his voice hushed as if he were entering a cathedral.

"Nobody got out if that's what you're hoping," Floyd said. "The guys have been working for a few months on the big rewiring project. Lifting grates, ripping out ceilings, and then repurposing and adding abatements. Like Trey said, we got some high-voltage wiring down here, though, so don't stand around touching pipes or nothing."

Something was not as right as Trey had hoped it would be. He had anticipated that Rob Fallon would just be here hiding, maybe playing with himself or even hurting himself, which he'd sometimes done.

"Why'd this guy come down here anyway?" Cameraman Carl asked, shining his light in the dim room far below, which took on a greenish cast from the lights above. Water dripped from heavy pipes that ran along the walls and ceiling.

"Who knows? He saw an opportunity," Trey said.

"He wants to escape," Lance whispered.

"What?" Jim Anderson asked as if this were the most lame-brained thing he'd ever heard.

"I always do my research," Lance said. "I know a patient got out through here about ten or twelve years ago."

"That ain't true," Jim said. "There's no way."

Trey put his hand on Jim's shoulder. "Yeah, someone tried to. Didn't get far. But somehow made it out to the middle of Jackman Boulevard."

"Pipes," Lance said, pointing to the wide green pipes of the ceiling. "The wiring guys told me some of those tunnels caved in over the past thirty years. You follow the big green pipes and eventually you're somewhere just outside the fence. It's impossible to get through there now, though. It's all clogged up."

"I know Fallon too well," Trey said. "He's not interested in escape, believe me. It's more likely he's just down here playing with himself."

"I don't feel great about this," Carl said, lowering his camera. "Lance, look, let's just stay up top here."

"We're getting the stories of Darden," Lance said. "Now, switch it to low-light and keep it on your shoulder."

"I don't want chatter down there, unless it's me, Jim, or Floyd. Got it?"

"Yes, sir," Lance said without much humor in his voice.

Trey looked over at Floyd, who remained back a ways, as if he didn't want to look down into the underground area known by most staffers as the Pit.

Floyd leaned against the wall, his sight wandering from door to door and then back again. *Floyd must hate this part of his job.* Trey didn't even like to admit to himself how creeped out he was about going down these stairs into the underground tunnels and warrens.

"Robby's smart," Jim said. "Holy crap, look at that." He shined his flashlight over in a corner.

A pile of dead rats, their stomachs ripped open.

"I guess the rat poison worked," Floyd said.

"Poor little guys," Jim said. "I know it's soft of me, but I hate seeing dead animals. Even rats. I like rats."

"But not in the food," Floyd said, and Trey was sure he heard the familiar smack of gum again coming from the guard's mouth.

3

By the time they reached the bottom step, Nelson's hand had begun trembling enough for Trey to notice. "It's okay, Floyd. It's Fallon. He doesn't bite like some of the others."

"Not unless you get cozy with him," Jim added.

When Trey stepped down onto the floor, the planks creaked. The floors were made of slats of wood raised over a stone and concrete surface. Not the original wood, but a more recent addition, mainly raised up because of flooding that occurred now and then when the rains came through Southern California.

At the floor level, Trey noticed the smell more than anything. It was an awful mix of mustiness and mildew and even the rotting rats, as well as something that reminded him of a swamp. He never liked thinking about the underground when he was above it. He felt it was part of the shame of Darden's past—back when, instead of medication, they used what now seemed like medieval tortures on the patients. He didn't like thinking about the kind of asylum Darden was in the late nineteenth and early twentieth century. Whenever people bemoaned the use of medication or the compassion of modern-day criminally insane hospitals, he wished they had seen the evidence he had of the past: of the operating rooms, the treatment facilities, and the cells that were known as "night cages" by the patients themselves because they were kept in isolation and darkness.

4

Trey walked ahead of the others, shining his light into the dimmer areas. The overhead lights were unstable, flicking in the main entry foyer, which was nothing more than a big empty room with a cracking wood-slat floor and exposed wiring and pipes all along its walls. Straight ahead, the first corridor down and to the left, was a large room-length square hole where a window had once been. Inside, old file cabinets, a pile of rubble and another pile of tools left by the construction and repair crews that came down occasionally. He didn't like to anticipate fear. Not in his work, not in his life. His wife had told him, "Don't die twice," and it was a huge lesson for him about dealing with fearful situations. He knew she had meant, "Don't suffer before you have to," and he tried to apply that whenever faced with situations that raised the hackles of his old fears.

But since the Red Angel killer—a man who was now a heavily medicated patient in Ward D—Trey had begun having nightmares about work and life that had not subsided. What bothered him the most was that sometimes, when he woke from the dreams, he wondered if patients at Darden State didn't experience the same sense of dislocation and anxiety that he felt. He had heard about it happening—a certain confusion when working so closely with the criminally insane population, sociopaths, especially.

"They get inside you," Dr. Brainard had told him years before. "And you have to do what you can in life to leave this place behind every day you walk out that door. Because once you stop leaving it behind, once you take Darden State with you, it's too late. You are no longer helping the patients. You're becoming one of them. And you'll start self-medicating. You'll begin to hallucinate in the same way the patient does. It's the close working quarters that do it, and I can't advise anyone to stay on the psychiatric technician staff for more than fifteen years. I think it's a mistake to make this your life's calling."

It had been bad for Trey before. When Agnes Hatcher had escaped a while back, he'd gotten caught up in her delusions to some extent. And with the Red Angel killer, he'd had images in his mind he'd never be able to erase: the memories of the most horrifying thing he'd yet experienced in life. He could name patient after patient who'd had no effect on him—terrible murderers, sociopaths, psychopaths. But something of his feeling of safety had eroded in the past year, despite his new position at Darden and his consulting work with Jane Laymon.

He had begun to believe too much in the nightmare, and not enough in the positives of life.

Being in the underground did little to brush away these fears.

But with a reporter and cameraman nearby, he wasn't about to mention it. He took a few deep breaths, and toggled a light switch near the entrance to the corridor as they all stood before its darkness.

"Let there be light," Jim said, like a voice of comfort beside him, as the flickering fluorescents above them came up.

CHAPTER FOURTEEN

1

"This is the back way. The main entrance is at the opposite side. It's completely sealed off from the grounds above," Jim Anderson said. "Twenty rooms on this level, twenty-five below."

Lance Victor looked down at his feet, then back at the others. "Below? There's another floor underneath this?"

Trey nodded. "They used to call it the bunker. But before that, they were the cages."

"Night cages. That's what they called 'em. They kept them all there," Jim added.

"Loonies," Floyd said. Floyd Nelson still hadn't quite gotten the hang of calling the patients by their more politically correct designations.

"People who were ill," Trey corrected him. "Back then, it wasn't a forensics hospital. They weren't all murderers. Patients with tuberculosis were housed in the same area as those who were violent schizophrenics, and beside them were sociopathic killers, and in the next bunk might be a woman who had been put there by her husband just because she was menopausal."

"Gay men and women, too," Jim said. "Just because they were homosexual and somebody with power over them put them here. Shock treatments. Insulin-induced shock. Thoracic surgery. And all of them having to live together. Before meds. Well, before really effective meds."

"Sounds like a torture chamber," Lance said.

Trey glanced back at him. Lance Victor kept back a ways, and Carl, his eye behind the camera, moved it around to take in the sights of the hallway.

"It's got some kind of night vision?" Trey asked. "That camera?"

"Yeah. It can get a reasonably decent image with almost no light at all."

"With luck, the lights'll come up as we go. But if they don't, I may have to ask you to use it to look around in the dark."

"Sure," Carl said, his voice utterly serious.

"The few times I've been down here, I always get the heebie-jeebies," Trey said.

"Makes me want to just go back upstairs and wait for this guy to come up on his own," Jim said.

"Knowing Rob," Trey said, "he's terrified right now. Poor guy."

And that's just what he was—they had followed the old corridor down past the empty administrative offices, past where any light reached, and they found

Rob Fallon nearly shivering under one of the old operating tables.

Trey stood at the entrance to the room. It was a medical theater, although not particularly large, with seating for about ten on a raised platform that overlooked the room and its three metal tables.

"Rob, it's okay. You can come out," Trey said, shining his flashlight near Rob's hand, which stuck out from beneath the table.

"I can't," Rob said, his whisper echoing in the chamber.

"It's okay. We'll just go back up and get settled."

"She brought me down here," Rob said.

"Who?" A shock went through Trey. Had someone else come down here with Fallon? Had Fallon managed to seduce another female employee?

"The girl," Rob said.

"Where is she?"

"By the door."

Trey shone the light in the doorway below them.

"There's no one there."

"That's what she wants you to believe."

"Let's go back up," Trey said. "Maybe she'll come with us." He motioned to Jim and Floyd to step back quietly. Then Trey leaned over the railing and turned about, hanging over the edge of it, his flashlight between his teeth. He jumped the few feet down, landing in a crouching position.

Rob Fallon scooted back under the operating table.

Trey walked to the doorway and found the light switch. He flicked it up. *Thank God it works.*

The white glow of the light came up, accompanied by a buzzing sound. The light began flickering overhead almost immediately.

Above, on the platform, both Floyd and Jim stood still, watching. Behind them, obeying all the rules set out for them, were Lance and his cameraman.

Trey crouched down again, looking at Fallon.

Beneath the table, Fallon looked like a young bird tossed too early out of the nest. Weak, hungry, frightened. Not the murderer who had torn the face off a woman and chopped her up, back in his early twenties. Not the same one who had raped and murdered his own mother.

His face was pale white and shiny with sweat.

"Who is she?" Trey asked.

"She's here," Rob said, glancing around, his voice a whisper. "I can feel her."

"Is she from Darden?"

He nodded.

"Is she a nurse?" Trey felt dread as he asked the question, fearing that Rob had lured someone here and had killed her.

He shook his head. "She's a little girl. A little girl. And she told me terrible things about this place."

Trey crawled closer to Fallon, putting his hand out. "Come on, Rob, it's all right. Just take my hand and come out. We can go upstairs. You can watch TV or get some rest."

Fallon looked at Trey's hand, and then looked over Trey's shoulder as if searching for someone. Trey resisted the urge to turn around. He had to keep his eye contact square with Fallon's, although it was best not to look Fallon directly in the eyes. Better to look a little off to the side so that Fallon would not begin to see Trey as the enemy.

"I think she's lived down here a long, long time," Fallon said.

"Give me your hand, Rob." Trey extended his arm as far as it would reach. He needed to be close enough for Rob to take his hand, but far enough away should Rob suddenly attack—which was not unusual for the patients in Ward D.

If Rob went into hyperspeed, Jim and Floyd would have about twenty seconds to get down in that pit with him and wrestle Fallon off him. Despite Fallon's slight build, he was like a mountain lion when he attacked.

Trey's fingers brushed the tips of Rob's fingers.

Trey felt his mouth go dry. *Come on, Robbie. Give it up. Let's not have any trouble.*

Rob's eyes went wide suddenly, as if there really were someone standing behind Trey, and when Trey felt a gentle whisper of air on the back of his neck, he twisted around for just a second. Nothing was behind him, just the suggestion had given him that feeling— but it was too late. Rob had already grabbed his hand, and pulled him fast beneath the table. Trey began trying to hold Rob's arms back, but Rob, using teeth and hands and legs and even his head—banging it against Trey's—became relentless in the attack.

Trey felt claws rake across his face as he did everything he could to gain the advantage, but it wasn't until Jim and Floyd had gotten down into the operating pit with him that they were able to pull Rob Fallon back, and hold him in a four-point star—a man on the legs, another on the arms and shoulders, and another to hold his chin back so that he couldn't use the strength in his spine to get free.

"Hey buddy, good going," Jim said, panting as he looked down at Trey, who had Rob's legs and pelvis pressed against the floor. "You still got your eyes."

2

After they called for a nurse to come down with a dose of Cambex, and Rob got a nice shot in the butt of the fastest sleep aid known to Darden, they carried Rob back up into Ward D. "Jesus, it's like we're croc hunters. I'm Steve Irwin today," Jim said. "We'll be on TV. Crikey!"

"My kid loves that show," Trey said. "I have to keep him from grabbing snakes when we go hiking."

After they got Rob settled nice and snug in some restraints in his cot, he began muttering something about wanting to kick some serious psych tech ass as he drifted off into med-induced oblivion. Floyd Nelson stood in the doorway to the room and said, "That was one creepy place down there."

Trey glanced back at him. "You lock it back up?"

3

"You know what, chief?" Jim asked. They'd left Rob Fallon's room, and were headed back down the hall to the door to the underground after making sure that

Lance Victor and Carl-the-Camera-Guy had gone off in search of another docudrama treasure for his series.

"What?"

"You're an anal son of a bitch."

"You say that so happily," Trey said.

"Of course the guy locked it up."

"I think Floyd was freaked by all the stuff down there."

"Floyd and Lance Victor both," Jim said. "Carl the cameraman seemed to be cool as a cucumber, though. I guess they expected it to be more like a basement of horrors."

"I get freaked down there, too. But I need to make sure."

When they reached the entry to the underground, Trey pulled at the door, checking the lock.

"See? Floyd's on top of this stuff."

Trey withdrew the keys from his pocket, unlocked the door and opened it.

The green and red stairway lights were still on. Trey gave Jim a knowing look, reached around to the switch, and shut them off.

He looked down into the darkness.

Then he stepped back and shut the door again.

Locked it. Locked the bolt.

It didn't make Trey feel any better, knowing that some workmen would be going down there again before evening. They couldn't have a guard on the door every second of the day, not with the reduction in the number of correctional officers since the budget cuts the previous spring.

4

In his office, going through Mary Chilmark's files, Trey heard a slight tap at the open door. He glanced up.

Floyd Nelson stood there, leaning against the door, as if he'd been watching Trey for awhile.

"Come on in," Trey said. "What's up?"

"Just a question. About that place."

"Sure. Some of the old-timers can probably tell you more about it. Marshall was part of the relocation crew in '53."

"Why do they keep it like that? I asked some of the guys, but nobody seems to know. I mean, beyond using it for storage and maybe for the rewiring job."

"Oh," Trey said, grinning slightly. "You mean the tables and the offices and stuff?"

"It looks like . . . well, it looks bizarre."

"Some wise-ass administrator found out it was cheaper just to let it all rot down there than to do anything about it. I think it's called 'administrative atrophy.'"

"Yeah, but in some of those rooms . . . hell, I saw a supply room that looked like it still had . . . all kinds of shit in it. Medical stuff."

"Old useless medical crap, probably. You might not want to dwell on it too much," Trey said. "We live above it in the sunshiny world of our hospital, and below us is that pit. Well separated, I'm told, by a ton of pipes and insulation and all kinds of grids that keep us from sinking. I'm sure Willard or some board member's eventually gonna clear it out or they'll fill it in like they did with the north wing. They bulldozed in a lot of dirt and rocks and concreted over part of it to the north—right over the field out by the fence. I bet Alice in B's got the files on the whole thing if you want to look it up. Floyd? You okay? Look, here." Trey went to his side desk, with the files, and drew them out. "I have a cool centennial book on Darden." He brought out a thin magazine-size paperback. On the cover was what looked like a gothic castle. "See, this is the above-ground part, circa 1906. They tore it down for a newer building in 1963, but this one went all the way down to the cells."

"You ever get freaked out by being here?" Floyd asked.

"Unofficially? Sure," Trey said. "All the time. You got to develop some gallows humor about this place to get through it. What about you? You were at Chuck-awalla."

"It was rough," Floyd said, a shadow seeming to cross his face. "But this is a different kind of rough. There, you knew who the mean ones were. You expected them. Here, you just can't tell. Sometimes . . . sometimes when I do my rounds, I think they all just seem like nice people."

"Until they try to bite your tongue out," Trey said, trying to get the guard to laugh. When Trey's phone rang, Floyd waved goodbye and went back out the door. Trey picked up. "Campbell, D."

"You called me earlier. I'm calling you back," Dr. Brainard said.

CHAPTER FIFTEEN

1

Brainard's office was upstairs, at the end of the east wing. You entered it first through safety doors—those double-thick steel doors that shut like a trap if even one alarm sounded in the building. It was a suite of offices used by the on-staff psychiatrists who did not keep outside offices. Outside each office was a cubicle for the psychiatrist's assistant. The floor had a beautiful Persian carpet runner, and the smell in the air was of coffee and roses. There was a reception area with a woman named Lara behind the counter, working the phones and the general assignment board, where staff supervisors arrived to check on any med changes authorized.

Lara hadn't been at Darden long, but had managed to get to know everybody by their first name within her first three months. "Hey, Trey, how ya doin'?"

"I'm here to see Dr. Brainard."

Lara smirked. She didn't have to say what she was

thinking—*He's in a mood. Be careful.* She readjusted her headset, pressed a button on the phone. "Diego? Is he in? Trey Campbell's here for him. All right. Thanks." She pulled her headset off and set it next to her coffee mug. "He's making you wait. You know that."

"I expected it. What's the word up here?"

"Well, that TV guy was with Hannafin early, right when she came in. I think she's milking the whole thing. I think I caught a little whiff of jealousy up here about it."

"Naw, they're behind her 100 percent. She can do no wrong," Trey said. "Besides, I heard her book was pretty good."

Lara reached under her desk, and drew up a copy of the hardcover. *The Killer Instinct: Inside the Minds of Seven Psychopathic Murderers.* She opened it to show him how far she'd gotten. "It's weird to think the guys she's describing are just one floor down and to the left. I practically feel like I've been reading their diaries."

"She doesn't name them, right?"

"No, but you don't need a name tag to figure out who they are. She has your pretty boy in here."

"Rob?"

Lara nodded. "Oh yeah. She calls him the Movie Star, like he's on *Gilligan's Island.* I heard you had an adventure with him today. Down under."

Trey grinned. "Word gets around."

"Well, I'm the one they all come running to with their secrets," she said. Then a buzzer went off on her phone. "Okay, well, it looks like it's time for you and Dr. B. Have fun."

Trey picked up the book, hefting it from one hand to the other. He turned it over and looked at the picture of Susan Hannafin. "Look at her. She's a star."

"Don't say anything bad about her. I love the book."

"Can I borrow it?"

"Get your own copy," she laughed. "I'm only on the third psycho."

2

Diego, Dr. Brainard's personal assistant was at the closed door to Brainard's office, at the very end of the hall. "He's in a mood," Diego said.

"So I gathered."

"I'm guessing you know why," the assistant said, and then opened the door into Brainard's office.

3

The office was the largest one Trey had seen inside the Ward. Sprays from green plants were at either side of the doorway, and the white carpeting had Persian rugs thrown over it just in front of his desk and farther back near a sitting area at the far end of the office. The filing cabinets were made of cherry, and the desk itself was enormous and curved around to provide an area for Brainard's assistant to come in and take dictation. On either end of the desk were two crystal vases with roses and lilies in them. On the wall, the requisite certificates and degrees, and pictures of Dr. Brainard through various decades with the famous and politically connected of California. On the bookshelf next to Brainard's desk, a handful of his own books, published over the past twenty-six years on the nature of the human mind and its psychiatric deviancies. On his desk, Dr. Hannafin's book, closed, looking as if it had never been opened.

Two green overstuffed leather chairs sat on the opposite side of the desk from Brainard himself.

Brainard, at his desk, glanced up from a stack of papers, as if surprised to see Trey Campbell at all.

4

Dr. Robert Brainard was a hard-ass of a psychiatrist, but Trey had developed some respect for him over the years. He had silver-gray hair, very thick and neatly trimmed, a longish face, and a slight indentation from some old scar just below his lip. Other than that, he was of the "handsome doctor" school: well-groomed, kept trim by morning trips to the gym, and was always dressed in a suit that looked like it cost a thousand bucks or more. He had an edge of class and the kind of condescending attitude that annoyed many, but not Trey. He knew it was a defense for some little dark corner of insecurity.

He also had steely blue eyes that seemed piercing at times.

Trey stepped in, shutting the door behind him. It was shadowy in the office; the blinds were drawn; the overhead lights were off, but an imitation Tiffany lamp on a corner table gave off a reasonable amount of light. Still, it was as if it were nearly dusk.

"I can give you ten minutes," Brainard said.

CHAPTER SIXTEEN

"It's about Mary Chilmark's son," Trey said.

Brainard leaned back in his chair, folding his hands over his chest. "Sure."

"Quentin Chilmark. In Program 28."

"I know. I signed the papers."

"I want to know about Mary Chilmark. His mother."

"It's all in the files. Surely, Dr. Hannafin—"

"With respect, sir, I've been assigned to do all intake and eval, with the supervision of Dr. Hannafin. I have been going over some of Mary Chilmark's files. Given that you were the psychiatrist who worked with her and signed her release evaluation, I thought you might be able to give me some insight that's not on paper."

"You know . . ." he paused slightly, a bit of bitterness creeping into his voice. "As involved as you are these days in matters of police and legal interest relating to our patients, you must never forget that they're patients. Quentin Chilmark is not in Program 28 today because we're going to spend time catching his mother for a homicide investigation."

"Sir, if I may." Trey opened the envelope in his hands and brought out a sheaf of papers. "In your exit evaluation, you said this about Mary Chilmark. 'The murders of two women, one man, and an unborn child. Each seemed to have an element of irony to the murder, for they were people who, in her original state, the patient felt had done some moral or spiritual wrong that needed to be brought back to them ten-fold.' I'd like to know what that meant."

"Mr. Campbell, it was a long time ago. I do not always recall the inflection of a patient's voice when reiterating psychosis. Particularly after twenty years and thousands of other patients who have become residents here."

"I know she murdered her victims in the hospital where she worked. San Pascal. I have pictures here . . ."

Dr. Brainard raised one hand slightly, his voice a little weary. "All right. I don't need to see them. I remember those pictures well enough."

Trey nodded and sat down in one of the chairs that faced Brainard's desk.

Brainard leaned forward, brushing his hand over some papers, and flicked on a small halogen desk lamp. An intense square of light hit the desk. Brainard reached up to rub his eyes and the bridge of his nose. "I'm not unaware of the connections that have been drawn between Mary Chilmark and myself. She was pregnant by some tech who worked with her at the time, but for some reason that wasn't glamorous enough for the staff. Because I spent a quarter of a year working with her—primarily because she was showing extraordinary progress—the rumors flew that I had fucked her."

Trey leaned forward in his chair, his hands nearly touching Brainard's desk. "That's not why I'm here. I want to know about her."

"I'm clearing the air, Campbell. I knew her well enough to know that she had become attached to me in a way I didn't think was healthy for her. I am willing to bet she's even convinced her son that I'm his father. When Dr. Massey married her—once she had been released—I felt that she had moved on successfully. It wasn't until his suicide that it crossed my mind she might have had a reversion of psychotic behavior. It was the death of her father that led her to murder those people in the hospital."

"That, and revenge."

"Revenge. Or not. It was trauma and repressed memory that triggered the event then. And if she has now—with her adult son—murdered, while it's not pleasant, it doesn't surprise me. I suspect Massey failed her."

"By killing himself?"

"Exactly. And don't raise those eyebrows, he did kill himself."

"Yes, sir. But the coincidence of both her father and her husband killing themselves . . ."

"I'm not saying that Mary herself may not have abused them both in some way. But their lives were taken by their own hands," Brainard said. "I should've seen the signs with Massey. He was a troubled soul if there ever was one. But I thought he had gotten on the right track. He resigned you know, after she left. He made a break and got into private practice."

"And then he killed himself."

"People do that now and then," Brainard said. "He was complex. She was, too. I have no doubt he loved her very much."

"How does it happen?"

"What—suicide?"

"No. How does a woman who kills three people—and at least with one of them, does something pretty nasty before the victim dies—get her time in Darden State completely cut?"

"You know how it works. She met the criteria."

"But she'd only been here two years."

Brainard shook his head. "You think this is quantifiable. It's not. We did our best by her. And it's not as if she went on a rampage after she got out of here. These current murders—which, I'll remind you, she's *allegedly* connected to, at this point—they're nearly twenty years after her time spent here. I have no idea what set her off, if indeed she was set off at all. We have her son here. He's the one we can talk to. But for all you know, Mary Chilmark is dead, too. Has anyone thought of that? Has anyone considered that her son may have killed her?"

Trey brightened a bit. "He says she's still alive."

"And he may be operating under delusional thinking right now. Are you playing detective here?"

"No, sir. I'm doing my job."

"Your job is made-up," Brainard said. "The state of California wants you here. Even the board members want you here. But I don't. I'm not happy about the way you handle the patients. A psychiatrist is murdered in the foothills because of her own stupidity, and you, along for the ride, get a promotion. My best advice to you is to find a more administrative position, and get away from the hands-on approach until you have full medical training."

Trey felt his hackles rise a bit at this remark, but tried to focus on the Chilmark case. "Sir, I don't care about rumors. I don't care about what you think of me or what you think of my promotion here. I respect your authority and your work. I just would like you to tell me about the murders she committed in the late 1970s."

"It's all in the files. But I guess with your new position here, I need to follow through or someone on the board will slap my hand. Mary came here when she was young and troubled. She was in her early twenties. Just out of nursing school. She was smart. She had graduated early from her program, top of her class. As I recall, she murdered a man who was seventy-four, a woman of twenty, and another woman who was pregnant. In my work with her—after she came to Darden, which was soon after her trial—she exhibited signs of molestation, trauma, and intense stress at the death of her father. She had precipitating incidents, including possibly the threat of rape, and sometimes, Campbell, we all have a button. When that button gets pushed, it sends someone over the edge. Her button was pushed, and there was no fail-safe for her. Additionally, she had attempted suicide a few years earlier, although this was not known until we found the scars on her body. As we worked with her, she became not only a model patient, but began showing remorse for the murders," Brainard said. "She told me that the old man had reminded her of her father. When she took him his medication one night, he had begun fondling her. This triggered the event that led to his murder. And unfortunately, she also went out of control that night. The others were killed as well, although in some respects, they were bystanders in the hospital to main killing. Certainly, it was with the old man that she got her most . . . well, creative is a word I hate to use."

"Not so creative," Trey said. "She cut off his testicles and penis, and put them in his mouth. He bled to death."

Brainard wore a grim look. "She was in the height of her psychosis. She had been raped repeatedly as a girl. She had been tormented and tortured by her father. A repeat victim of incest of the worst type. Her degradation was constant and her father was responsible. And yet his death triggered feelings of guilt and fury. Trey, you know by now how this often goes. Psychosis meets abuse meets trauma meets opportunity to act out. It's not always in such a neat package, but this one was practically textbook."

"I understand. So she took revenge on the man in the hospital for his sexual advances by castrating him. But why in the mouth? What's that about?"

Brainard stood and went over to the windows. He raised the blinds. Outside, a haze of light. "She liked the punishment to fit the crime. That was part of her behavioral deviance. But she got beyond it. Through therapy and work, she responded, Trey. At least . . . at least it appeared that way at the time." Brainard wiped his face with his hands as if he could somehow take the mood away. "I will say this. She was an extraordinarily sexual creature. Her appetite was enormous, which made us wonder if the traumatic episodes had not awakened a part of her brain. She could not seem to shut it off. Thus, her advances to the staff—and to me, yes—were constant. It could not simply be explained by acting out. She was seductive to the extreme. She knew that she was a beauty, and she did everything but unzip flies. I always brought two female nurses in whenever I met with her. Even so, she knew how to give subtle sexual hints of her availability."

"I doubt that poor old guy in the hospital ever touched her," Trey said.

"There was evidence to the contrary, of course," Dr. Brainard said, a slightly disappointed tone in his voice. "Look, Campbell. Her past history is there. It's in the files. You're welcome to them. We don't know who the father of that boy was, and I've always assumed it was Dr. Massey."

"That one still baffles me," Trey said. "He married her after he got her out."

"Yes."

"Until he took his own life five years ago. And yet this seemed to trigger nothing in her. No incidents reported. She lay low and was quiet. How well did you know Massey?"

"Not well enough. He was a troubled man. Sometimes those who enter the psychiatric field do so primarily because they are deeply troubled," Dr. Brainard said. "Some of us are here out of genuine curiosity of the mind, while others are here because it was their training, and still, now and then, a man like Dr. Massey will show up who has spent his life studying the mind and its psychoses because he does not have a handle on himself. When he told me he wanted to . . . well, take care of her on the outside, I assumed that baby was his. But it might not have been. Maybe it was another patient here. A tech or an orderly. Anybody. We may never know. But despite her sexual proclivities, she met all the criteria for release. And, per the law, we could not keep her if the board felt she would benefit from release. You weren't around then, but some very progressive judges were looking over cases like Mary's, and she met every one of their checklists as a good candidate for continuing therapy and reintegration into the outside world."

Trey remained silent. Seconds ticked by on the wall clock—it was nearly noon.

Dr. Brainard half grinned, like a man who remembered his youth much better than it ever could be. "I was fresh out of my first internship, and came here to help these people. I hope I have. I hope I continue to do so. She was different. She didn't even look like the other patients. She seemed healthy and vibrant, and sometimes . . . sometimes when I spent time with her, I felt as if she were a psychologist sitting there, talking to me. Intelligent. Curious. Not at all like a patient or a prisoner." Brainard shook his head. "I just can't believe she's regressed to this point. I mean, she hasn't had a history since leaving here. Not 'til today. Are they sure her son didn't act alone?"

Trey nodded. "Yes. Even Doc Chilmark puts himself there with her."

"Doc?"

"Her son. His name's Quentin, but he goes by Doc.

He thinks he's a natural healer. He claims she acted as his nurse for the operation."

"He may be lying."

"I don't think he is. I don't think he cares. He believes he did the right thing by the woman and her baby."

Something changed in Brainard's demeanor. He suddenly looked as if he had some insight that hadn't occurred to him before. "With that man in the hospital. Back then. She cut off his penis and testicles and stuffed them in his mouth and stitched his lips together. She said she did it so he'd know what it felt like, too. What she'd felt like having him want to put it in her mouth. Is there something about this murder like this? Some kind of warped poetic justice?"

CHAPTER SEVENTEEN

1

As soon as he'd left Brainard's office, Trey went out to the grounds and opened his cell phone. Jane Laymon picked up after two rings. "The Flocks knew the Chilmarks. Somehow. They had some relationship with them."

"Nobody seems to be able to put them together. I wonder how they interacted."

"I don't know. But they had to. Tell me exactly what was done to the bodies."

Jane catalogued the murder scene for him: the way the woman was cut open. The blood. The man was first attacked on the stairs, but likely was not meant to be the victim. He had simply surprised them. If he'd come home an hour later, he'd be alive.

The woman was the intended victim.

She had done something to Bloody Mary and Doc.

They had exacted their revenge in some way.

2

Trey went back to the room with Doc Chilmark. Doc looked too comfortable in his straitjacket and hobbles.

"How did you know Mrs. Flock?" Trey asked.

"I don't know nobody with that name."

"Your mother. How did she know her?"

"My mother is a nurse. She knows when people are sick."

"But you're a doctor," Trey said. "Don't you know?"

"Not always. Sometimes a nurse knows more than a doctor. Everybody knows that's true. Sometimes doctors can be very, very blind to things."

Trey kept his eyes on the young man. In restraints, sitting up in his cot. Then Trey got up and left the room.

3

In the hall outside Chilmark's room in Program 28 the guard, Atkins, stood by.

"Why's he still in a jacket?" Trey asked.

"Every time we take it off, he goes for the balls."

"His or yours?"

Atkins chuckled. "I don't care if he goes for his. It's mine I'm thinking about."

"I want the restraints off."

"With respect, I think that's unwise, Trey."

"We can bring in some more officers if you feel the need for protection. There's no reason for him to have that straitjacket and the hobbles on in there. The only reason for it would be if he hurt himself in some way."

"Can I ask why?"

"He's too comfortable in that straitjacket. He likes being bound up. I want him a little uncomfortable for a while."

Atkins's expression soured. "Okay. Well, we're gonna need some heavy hitters. Let's get Anderson, Jarrett, and Schwartz down here. If this gets into take-down territory, I assume you'll accept responsibility."

"Completely," Trey said. "Let's do it."

4

Twenty minutes later, three more beefy guys showed up. Jim Anderson was among them with a big smile.

"Five guys with a nineteen-year-old. I think we should be able to keep this together," Trey said.

He unlocked the door to Chilmark's room.

Inside, Chilmark had already taken the straitjacket off.

5

"It's an old trick," Chilmark said once Trey had entered the room again. "When I was little I loved Houdini. He was into ghosts and séances, just like me. He could escape from anything. Straitjackets are easy. I have a jacket like this at home. When I was little, when I was bad, my mother would put me in it. She told me it was so I wouldn't hurt myself." The cadence of his voice had a chilling effect on Trey, and he felt that the guards with him must've felt it, too. Chilmark was too relaxed. It was nearly as if another personality had come out from him. Nothing threatening. Nothing worrisome, but a completely different aura to his tone and the slight grin he wore. It was as if he were playing a part for them.

"Okay. Okay, so you can do the amazing escape trick. Why didn't you do it before?"

"I wanted to impress you," Chilmark said. He grinned. "Well, plus I don't mind the jacket."

"I know, Doc. You feel good in it."

"I like this place," Chilmark said. "It feels like a calm place. Not like that other place."

"What other place? The Flocks' house?"

"That was awful." Chilmark lost his smile. "Awful. I couldn't stand the light outside. The shadows. It all came crawling at me."

"What crawled at you?"

"They're like spiders sometimes. Crawling, crawling. From shadows outward. They like to bite when they touch you."

"Spiders?"

"Not spiders. Like spiders. The fears. The fears come at you. They crawl and they hiss and they come from a very bad place. Very bad." As Chilmark spoke, Trey felt the level of tension in the room rise.

"It's all right now," he said. "It's okay, Doc. You're here. Right here. No fears around. No shadows."

Chilmark took a deep breath and when he breathed out, he groaned. "If you take a breath and count to four before you exhale, you can make them go away. Sometimes."

"Why do they come?"

"The fears are there after healing. The ghosts move on, but the fears they leave behind start wanting to find someone else to get inside. You know about night fears?"

Trey nodded.

"No, you don't." Chilmark chuckled nervously, clapping his hands together. "You don't even know how many you have. But I know how many I have around me. In the dark."

"How many do you have?"

"Oh, thousands. Thousands and thousands, but they can't get in me. No, no, no. They want to, though. All the healing releases them. And they're waiting for me at night. They want me to close my eyes, but when it's dark out I always keep my eyes open. Always. When that lady got healed, and I saw her shadow go off to heaven, I knew that she left behind fears. Nothing you can do about that. Fears always stay back and they want to make a nest under your skin. That's what they do. They dig under your skin with their sharp little claws—teeny tiny so you can feel them but you can't see them at all—and they want to get inside you so they can do all kinds of things to you and eat you up from the inside out. That's what they do. They eat at everything under your skin. But I don't let them in me. No fears have gotten into me. They all wait to try to get under my skin. But they haven't gotten in yet. Well, once. But my mother destroyed them for me. You see how she did it? She did it right," he said, pointing to the streaks of scars along his face. "They got under my skin, nearly a hundred of them, but she went in with her cutters and she got them all out and if I don't sleep at night, they can't get back in me."

Trey let him calm down before returning the conversation to the murder. "Let's talk about the Flock family."

"Who?"

"You operated on a woman who had a baby inside her."

"It was a malignant tumor," Doc said. "She would've died with it in her."

"She's dead now."

"So you say. But I've seen her. Since. And she looked fine to me."

"How well did you know her?"

"I didn't know her," Doc said, a mischievous look on his face as if he were playing some kind of prank.

"Your mother knew her, then."

"You could say that." Doc grinned.

6

When Trey had gotten Atkins to unlock the door again, he brushed past him toward the double doors that separated Program 28 from the rest of Ward D. He walked swiftly down the hallway and opened his cell phone. He tapped in a number, waited; Jane Laymon picked up.

"Okay," she said. "Look, meet me at the morgue. It might help to see the handiwork. If you're ready. You sure you're up for this?"

"I'm not. But Bloody Mary is out there somewhere. And she might be ready to kill someone else," he said, and tried not think of Carly at work or at home or going to the post office, pregnant, the way Diane Flock had been pregnant. Just having an ordinary day at the very moment someone decided to torture her—and her unborn child—to death.

CHAPTER EIGHTEEN

1

The morgue in San Pascal was across town, but there was no traffic on the freeway, and he managed to avoid the red lights on the streets up to it. He parked, and Jane was already there at the automatic doors in front of the sheriff's building. She looked grim but still managed to smile when she saw him. Once inside the building, a slender man of fifty or so came up to the two of them, and Jane made introductions. "Trey, this is Howard Dahl. He's our lead investigator."

"Good to finally meet you, Mr. Campbell," Dahl said, shaking his hand vigorously, continuing to walk with them toward the stairs down to the morgue. "Laymon's told me she prepped you on the murders already."

"Yes," Trey said, noticing the smell of alcohol and bleach that wafted up from the staircase below.

"What she probably hasn't mentioned yet," Dahl said, "is that there was another murder. Only nobody thought it was a murder until we found some evidence linking it to the Flocks."

2

Trey had put on a surgical breathing mask, both because of the chemicals in the vicinity and the stink of the corpses. The smells were unavoidable at the morgue, no matter how well the ventilation system worked and no matter how low the temperature of the rooms. The lights overhead were nearly blinding if Trey looked up from the table, and they afforded the corpse on the table a glistening white glow, almost as if it were an alabaster sculpture rather than human flesh.

And it was not one of the Flocks. They were on separate tables toward the far end of the room.

This was a victim that had not been thought of as a victim.

Until now.

3

"His name's Cooper Fenn, and he lived in a trailer park. The body was found a day before the Flocks' murders. He was a well-known drunk in three counties for causing brawls, and he had warrants out for his arrest for everything from traffic violations to bounced checks to petty theft. Nobody was surprised when he was found dead," Dahl said. Then he looked at Trey and grinned. "You doing okay?"

"What? Sure." But even as he said this, Trey realized that he was sweating up a storm. His throat had gone dry.

"You look a little clammy," Dahl said.

Jane touched Trey's shoulder. "Maybe this was a mistake."

"No," Trey said. "It's okay."

"Sometimes the smells are a bit much. You open a body, and there's a lot of nastiness in it," Dahl said.

Get hold of yourself, Trey thought. *It's okay.*

But it was like the nightmares he'd had. The bright light. The pale skin of the dead. The dead man looking nothing like anyone Trey had ever seen. It was the downside of his new position: He had to get used to death. He had to see things as these investigators did. But something within him resisted, and he longed for his home and his kids and his wife and all the things that reminded him of a happier world.

"It's okay," Trey repeated. "So what ties this guy in with the Chilmarks and the Flocks?"

Dahl glanced first at Jane, then at Trey. Then, down to the corpse. "Here's the thing with Mr. Fenn here. He died apparently of natural causes, at least for him. Blood alcohol level was through the roof—point five oh, basically. So, sure, that's death. Only problem was, he's two hundred seventy-seven pounds at five-foot-four, and he'd survived alcohol poisoning in the past. Not to say he couldn't have died from it, anyway. That's certainly what everybody thought. But then the coroner's assistant found this." Dahl reached to the dead man's lips with his latex-gloved hands. Using two fingers, he drew the man's mouth open.

"You'll have to move a little closer to see this," Dahl said.

Trey leaned down. He breathed through his mouth, and felt queasiness in his stomach. Inches from the corpse's face, Trey saw the inside of the mouth.

The gums were swollen toward the back of the mouth.

"He's got eight teeth missing—someone pulled them. Now sure, maybe he was drunk and went crazy and pulled them himself," Dahl said, drawing his fingers out. "But we found the teeth. We didn't really know whose they were at the time."

"At the Flocks' house," Jane said.

"Perfect matches," Dahl continued. "So then, we come back to Fenn here, and we feel like we didn't study him enough."

"Let's not show it," Jane said. "I think Trey's just hanging in here."

"I'm fine. Let's do this. What else?"

Dahl stepped over to Cooper Fenn's thighs, and drew his legs apart. "Twelve eight-inch needles here. Maybe more. Once we get the X rays done, we'll know. Thrust up beneath his scrotum."

4

Afterward, sitting in Jane's car, Trey leaned back in the seat and took a sip of Starbucks coffee Jane had nabbed for him.

"Near as we can tell," she said. "They got him so drunk that he died of alcohol poisoning. But some-one—one of the Chilmarks—spent a lot of time carefully pushing these needles up inside him. After that, some of our guys searched Fenn's trailer. Because he had died out on the street, and everybody assumed it was whiskey or meth, nobody bothered to do a thorough search of his place. Just about an hour ago, they found that Doc Chilmark had lived with Fenn for four years. Everybody in the trailer court thought they were father and son. Nobody who has been interviewed so far knows what happened to Doc after the age of fourteen, but someone did say they thought his mother came and got him then. And that's when we figured out how Mary knew the Flocks."

"How?" he asked.

"In his past life, before the drinking got too heavy, Fenn had been an unlicensed acupuncturist. He ran a somewhat legit massage parlor down on Harland Avenue for years. It's gone now, but the people in the trailer talked about how good he was at massage therapy. Acupressure, Swedish, deep-tissue massage. He apparently did pretty good."

"Legit massage?"

"No idea. But Fenn brought out the acupuncture needles now and then when he thought somebody needed them. The business was a little off-the-books. I think Mary was working for him in that massage parlor. I think Mary went to Diane Flock's house because she got called in to do a massage. Diane let her in. Maybe she expected the son, too. Or maybe Mary worked on her own, and let her son in once she had Diane Flock subdued. We're doing some checks at area medical offices to see if she left her business card around."

"Nobody on that street saw those two?"

"Sometimes," Jane said, "in the light of day, people just aren't looking for murderers. How's Doc doing?"

"He's practically in heaven at Darden," Trey said. "He feels a connection to the place. I've never seen a patient adapt so well that quickly."

"Fenn's trailer park is in Caldwell, just over the ridge from Darden State. Mary Chilmark and her son might just have been living within a ten-minute drive of the hospital."

5

The call came in later, and Jane heard it replayed for her over the phone by Tryon, from a Mrs. Kilpatrick, who lived in Caldwell. "I'm a property owner and tax-payer and I think the woman they're calling Mary on the TV news is one of my renters. The picture on TV ain't exactly what she looks like, but that boyfriend of hers—no mistaking his mug."

Jane found the rental house where Bloody Mary Chilmark and her son, Doc, had lived for at least five years. It was on Third, right off Main Street with its strip of shopfronts that made up the nearly nonexistent town of Caldwell, California.

Less than a mile from Darden State.

CHAPTER NINETEEN

1

It was a scraggly little house with white shingles and an arched roof that nearly went flat over the box of house; it was set one dusty block behind Main Street and its bike shop, bank, markets, animal shelter, three bars, one with boarded-up windows, a Pep Boys, and the railroad tracks that crossed the road right in the heart of town. There were six houses on each side of the road, and then the side street dead-ended in a cul-de-sac. The driveway was mainly dirt with a thin veneer of crumbly pavement. Jane Laymon, who drove out alone to the place, parked in the street.

A thick-set woman of seventy with owl glasses and a white frizz of hair stood in the driveway looking as if she expected unwelcome relatives to show up. She wore a chambray workshirt and blue jeans. When Jane got out of her car, the woman took the magazine in her hand and held it over her eyes to block out the sun that had turned to red and black on the distant burning mountainside. "You a cop?"

"Detective Jane Laymon," Jane said, walking casually over to the woman. She drew her badge out for identification, and then put her hand out. "You're Mrs. Kilpatrick?"

"Mary-Louise," the woman said with the desert rat accent that was nearly Southern redneck, prevalent out along the dusty ridges of inland Southern California. Her face was that strange orange-brown of too much sun and too much age. Lines crossed and looped her skin like crop circles, making her look much older than the age she stated on the phone when Jane had been put in touch with her. "You should get yourself one of them glass eyes. Them eye patches draw attention."

Jane nodded. "I prefer a patch."

"I'm just sayin'. You're a pretty girl and all. What are you, six foot? They grow 'em tall where you come from, I guess."

"Yes, they do."

"All I'm sayin's I know a guy with a glass eye where you can't even tell he's got it until he pop it out and shows ya. His name's Ricky and he's sixty-three years old, and he pops it out and laughs at ya and it looks just like a real eye. I mean, a real eye with color and everything. Nobody'd know the difference, you ask me."

"Is this the house?" Jane asked.

"Yeah. I can't say nothin' too bad about her except she's a little long in the tooth to keep lookin' like she's twenty or something. She likes her men, I guess. Bad men, but she picked 'em, all's I'm sayin'. Best renter I got in other ways. Did all her own maint'-nance. When the driveway had cracks and holes all over it, she hired the guys to do it. Never once called me. She never complained. When the roof got a leak, she got up there and fixed it herself. She was that way."

"When was the last time you saw her?"

"She's been gone about a week. I come over every day," Mary-Louise Kilpatrick said. "I take in the mail. The papers. Check the lights. Make sure nothing's up. It ain't a bad neighborhood, but all's I'm sayin' is there's bad and there's good, and sometimes we got more bad on this block. It all comes outta L.A. They chase the gangs out this way—what, ten, fifteen years back. And now we got problems. She idn't like that. No riff-raff except that boyfriend. But when I went in today, somebody had got all the mail I had stacked up by the door. Maybe day before yesterday was when I saw it last. I take care of what I got. I own three of these houses." She pointed across the street and then to the house next door. "I don't never rent to no people without runnin' a credit check. I do a TRW and some-times that other kind. If they get late on their rent, they gotta go to Western Union down next to the Wienershnitzel and get a money order. I don't play no games. They owe, they owe. All's I'm sayin', I didn't have no trouble here. I had one of them Mexican fam-ilies tossed out, well, they just never were up to no good." Even as she said this, she glanced at Jane's face as if studying it. "You one of them?"

"One of what?"

"Mexicans? You look Mexican. Not that there ain't

good ones. They just don't live up here. We got Mexican cops now?"

Jane tried to forget the stink of beer in the air, a halo around Mary-Louise Kilpatrick.

"She's not here anymore," Jane said, confirming what Mary-Louise had said in her phone call to the police.

"Sometimes I seen her boyfriend around. That's why I made the call. But you people got him so I knew it was safe to go over."

"You went inside?"

"Well, I don't normally do it, but I just let myself in the back. And the place is a wreck. I cleaned up a little, knowin' you was comin'. I don't keep no pig style."

"Her name is Patty?"

"Patty's the renter, but it's her sister been livin' here for a while. Patty took off, but ya know, I don't care if it's one or th'other, I just care that they keep the place up and pay up. Payin' up is hard as hell for some of these folks. I had queer folks down the block, but they're pretty good with money just bad with sin, if you know what I mean. I mean, I'm a good Christian woman. We got the meth people near the end, by that house that got burnt out. We got some bad people. Patty, the sister, now she was good folk. Patty went to church over in Moreno Valley, but I told her that the Church of the Desert was a better place. But that sister of hers, she never went to any church I ever heard of."

"Mind if we go inside?" Jane asked.

"Don't see why not. Nobody home and she's three weeks behind on rent," Mary-Louise said. "I been worried sick about her since I saw the news."

2

Three eviction notices were taped to the front door. Mary-Louise snorted, as she turned the knob and opened the door, a step ahead of Jane. "She ignores them. Always late. I guess if Patty were here it would be easier, but that sister of hers. All's I'm sayin' is she don't like payin' rent. But she usually ends up comin' in just before I file with the court and I get a sob story about money bein' tight and then she pays me cash and we're good for another go 'round."

"What's Patty's sister's name?"

Mary-Louise did a half turn and took off her glasses, as if doing so would help her think better. "It's on the tip of my tongue. Can't quite get a hold of it."

"Did she ever write you a check?"

"I'd say yes, but I'd be lyin'. She was cash only."

"But she's the woman in the picture."

"Yeah, the one on the news. I knew that boyfriend of hers was up to no good."

"Boyfriend?"

Mary-Louise nodded her head, crossing one arm under the other, with her free hand touching the edge of her chin as if it helped her think. "He was a no goodnik. He was way too young for her, but women who stay single too long like she did, they invite that kinda trouble sometimes. Ya gotta marry young and stay married and then it all goes fine. But wait and wait and wait, and you end up with a guy half your age who'd as soon slit your throat as look at ya."

3

Inside the house, Jane first noticed the massage table, open, in the middle of the small living room. The shades were drawn. The room was furnished with things from the Salvation Army, or perhaps garage sales. Nothing matched, everything had a dinginess to it, and the lamp shades—as Mary-Louise went around turning the lights on—had blotchy stains on them. "I didn't know nothin' about her clients coming in here at all hours of the day and night. She said she was a nurse and a licensed masseur," pronouncing the word "masser," "and people's business ain't none of my own, but she was okay most times I saw her. But that man of hers. She was robbin' the cradle and then some, and he was into drugs or somethin' because he always looked shifty. Shifty eyes." She pointed to each of her eyes as she said it. "Shifty. Shady. He was never around and then he was suddenly there. If you ask me, she's the innocent one. Maybe she's a sinner, but he's the shifty one."

Jane went from room to room. In the tiny bedroom that was not much bigger than a closet she saw the dog crate. It was the size one might get for a German Shepherd or a Great Dane. "She had a dog?" Jane asked the landlady, who stayed back in the hallway.

"No, no critters. She was at least good about that. She couldn't stand animals. I swear I once saw her try to run down a cat that was just racing across the street."

Jane went over to the crate, crouching down beside it. The metal grid of the door was open.

A smell came from it, and she immediately thought of an animal.

But inside, there was a pillow, and a man's soiled underwear, size twenty-eight, and pushed to the very back, a pair of handcuffs.

4

After she'd radioed for two of her guys to show up and start a real inspection of the place, Jane went with the landlady out to the backyard. The back was concrete from the kitchen door out to the end of the property at a chain-link fence; beyond it, another house, nearly identical to this one. There was a plastic table under the roof overhang, and a couple of lawn chairs. On the table, an ashtray and a small bucket with a citronella candle in it. Jane walked out to the fence and looked between the houses in back—an alleyway ran between them, and there were two little girls playing with naked Barbie dolls. The clothes for the dolls were in a small pile.

Somewhere distant, a dog barked.

Jane glanced into the backyard of the house next door: a swing set, a children's play area that included a bright orange slide and a netted area for climbing. A barbeque grill, its top up.

She went back to the white plastic table by the kitchen door, where Mary-Louise sat. She'd already lit the citronella candle.

"When was the last time you saw her?" Jane asked.

"Well, she comes and goes. But I sit up waiting for her," Mary-Louise said. Then she pointed to Jane as if she were the tenant, "I say, 'You better pay me what you owe, missy, or I'm gonna call the sheriff and get you into court, you hear me?' And she's pretty good when that happens, and I get rent. But she's never this late, and when I saw her picture on TV, and that boyfriend's picture, I got a little afraid for her."

"Afraid her boyfriend had killed her?"

Mary-Louise nodded. "Mind if I light up?" She drew a pack of Salems from her jeans.

"Sure, go ahead."

"That boyfriend. I mean, he had that face. He had that look. It was like a pit bull, that guy was. I mean, not strong or anything. But he looked like he could go off on you any second. Luckily, I never saw him around here much. He killed those nice people over in San Pascal, didn't he?"

"He's been arrested."

"He's a kookooberry."

Jane raised her eyebrows.

"You know, koo-koo. Like you can feel it when he's around."

"Does she have friends in the neighborhood?"

Mary-Louise seemed a little taken aback that Jane didn't ask more about Doc Chilmark. She took a long drag off her cigarette, and blew a perfect smoke ring from between her lips. "Not friends as in friends. People seen her now and then. I guess you gotta ask around. I been on this block too long. I don't get to know nobody unless they get me my rent money. But I doubt anybody knew her. She was all quiet and I think a little ashamed of her business, having men in to give, well, what women *like that* give to men."

"You think she was a prostitute?"

"I never woulda had her here if I thought that!" Mary-Louise said, raising her cigarette up to eye level. "She wasn't bad like that. But she had *bad men*." She made this last point with midair jab of the cigarette. "That kookooberry boyfriend and some others. Any girl who rubs men down for a living ain't gonna get the guys you take home to mother, if you hear me. She was surrounded by badness. But she was a nice girl. I know she was. Patty woulda never let her stay there that long if she wadn't."

"Where's Patty now?"

"Eh, no idea." Mary-Louise sucked at the cigarette, and set it down in the ashtray. "Her mother got sick in Barstow and she took off to help with that stuff. Why that sister of hers wadn't back there helping, I don't got a clue. They was both nurses, so you'd a figured they'd trade off on that stuff. But Patty took off, and the sister—what's her name—?"

"Mary."

"No, that's not it, no, I'd never forget Mary, believe me. I know they called her that on the TV, and I guess that's what confused me. I kept seeing her picture and thinking, 'That's no Mary.' But it's one of those names that you don't forget, but look at me." Mary-Louise chuckled. "I'm too old to remember, too young to forget." She started snapping her fingers. "It's like a movie star name. Not movie stars now, but back when I was a girl. Jean. That's it—Jean something. Different last name than Patty, 'cause her husband left her. I got that much outta her before she started hidin' from me. Jean Kearney. Reminded me of Gene Tierney. Both the name and the way she looked. Like in that movie *Laura*. Ever see that one? It was good. That's who she looked like, a little. She had the teeth and the hair and that kind of glamorous look without even putting on too much makeup. Hard to believe that she and Patty were sisters, 'cause Patty was so plain, but you know, my older sister was the plain one and got the bad teeth and an inch too much nose that twisted a little to the left. So it happens. Patty was plain and bottle blond and musta had a hare-lip when she was little 'cause there was always this scar and the way she talked. Thometimeth thee talk like thith," Mary-Louise said, chuckling to herself as if she had done a perfect imitation of Patty. Jane was fairly sure now that Patty was probably buried somewhere, not far from here, while Mary Chilmark was still on the loose.

Mary-Louise lit another cigarette, took a swift puff off it, and said, "Well, seeing her and then seeing Jean, it was like night and day. That's why I didn't mind Jean being here. When she kept up with the rent. But that boyfriend of hers—he was bad news like you never heard bad news before in your life."

"What was Patty's last name?"

"Mullen. Patty Mullen. I used to think of her as Patty Sullen because she moped a lot. But she thought the world of that sister of hers."

5

Three cops showed up, and Dahl stood there in a gray suit as if he'd been pulled from an early dinner date.

Jane met them out front, warned them about Mary-

Louise, and said, "Kilpatrick's touched things in there, but I don't think it matters much. It's definitely Bloody Mary. Let's go over the place carefully, and maybe we can find out what her plans are."

"My guess is she's on the road," Dahl said.

"She loves her son too much," Jane said, shaking her head slightly. Then she looked out across the hills and the valley. The heat from the Santa Ana winds was blasting up a notch, and she had a taste of bitterness in her mouth. "I think she's nearby. I want officers to patrol the area here. The trailer where Fenn lived is two miles up the road, and Darden is just over that ridge. She's watching out for him now. She knows where he is. I think if we work fast, we can find her sooner than later."

Then she mentioned Patty Mullen and asked for a follow-up on her and her family in Barstow, to see if there might not be another murder on Bloody Mary's hands. "Chilmark went by the name Jean Kearney. Claimed to be Patty Mullen's sister. She ran the massage business out of her house but probably mainly did home calls. All her business was cash only. Let's find out if she had her business card in the local shops, or if anybody got to know her at all. We probably can't dig up her past clients on short notice, but maybe if we get the word out, they'll come forward."

CHAPTER TWENTY

Jane Laymon walked to her car and was about to get in, but decided she needed a walk instead. She went up the street to the end, by the cul-de-sac. The yards were unkempt, with splotchy yellow grass surrounded by dirt. Behind some of the chain-link fences, she saw a pit bull or a rottweiler or two. A child's tricycle had been left out at the end of one driveway, and the house at the end of the cul-de-sac looked like it had been burned at one point, perhaps years before. Its windows were boarded up. It obviously had been abandoned, so she stepped into the yard, and went to the back gate. She opened it and went out into a yard that looked like it was more desert than lawn. Local gang members and kids had spray painted their symbols all over the back of the house. The sliding-glass doors were broken, and trash of various kinds lay in piles under the shade of the roof. She went toward the back, where the fence had been cut, and pushed her way through it.

On the other side she saw a slight rise in a plateau barren of everything but tumbleweed and dried grasses. She went out into it, and when she came to the edge, not more than eight yards from the back of the house, she saw the valley beyond.

The hillside curved downward, and there, beneath where she stood was Darden State Hospital.

You watched it. Why? You and your son were here for years. Just watching the hospital. Waiting for what? For now? For the inevitable? Did you know he'd end up here? Or was that luck? You left the hospital, you got away with a new husband. You had your baby. You were fine for a time. And then things started to happen. What you'd kept away from your life began to come back. What happened? What was it that brought you back here six years ago to rent this house? Did you sit up on this hillside and look down at it like this? Were you here before you went to kill the Flocks? Before you killed Cooper Fenn? Were you here last night— thinking about your son—hoping he'd find his way back?

Jane stood there a long time, feeling the hot winds against her back, asking question after question in her mind. Having no answers.

And then different questions came to her. *What were you doing up here all those years? Between your first murders in your twenties, to the Flocks in San Pascal, and Fenn? Did you not have the desire to kill? Did someone cross you at some point, and you didn't hurt them? What were you doing up here, in this neighborhood? Giving massages to strangers. Letting men touch you. What triggered you now that didn't trigger you three years or ago or even six months ago?*

When she thought of possible answers, one struck her as utterly ridiculous.

But she couldn't ignore it.

You were killing then, too. Maybe not often. Now and then. When the madness got hold of you. When something awful happened. When you couldn't take it out on your little boy. When your husband had killed himself just to avoid you and the world he'd gotten involved in. Your deranged world where you lashed out at people like a rattlesnake when you felt they'd somehow intruded on your territory.

But if you were killing, why weren't there bodies before? You left the Flocks in their house. You left Fenn in his trailer. Where are the others, if there are others?

And then something came to her lightning fast, and the hot wind seemed to make her feel as if she were going to jump out of her skin if she didn't go see whether it was a possibility.

Without even realizing she was moving so fast, Jane began jogging back to the abandoned house, back down the street, back to the house that Mary Chilmark had been renting for several years.

Dahl was still there, and when she reached him, she said, "If there are bodies, they might be under the concrete in back. It's new. Kilpatrick said she didn't have to do any maintenance while Mary lived there. She told me that Mary even repaired the roof and hired workmen to redo the pavement in the driveway. I think she did the backyard, too. Men came here all the time for massages. Whatever triggered Mary to murder Diane Flock and her husband, that trigger may have been with her for years. Mary's husband killed himself

155

exactly five years ago. If that event triggered this, then my guess is she's been killing people since she moved up here. She just didn't hide the Flocks. Maybe she intended to but got interrupted by something. Maybe she didn't care."

"Maybe she wanted her son to get caught," Dahl said.

CHAPTER TWENTY-ONE

1

Mary Chilmark had spent the day sleeping with a very drunken Nick Spitzer, who wrapped his flabby arms all over her. But she felt safe with him, and she needed rest. Spitzer lived in a modest home near Belle-View Park, in the nicest part of Caldwell, and the country club—which was not quite as green as it should've been for that time of year—was just over the fence in his backyard. His wife had left him two years earlier, and had cleared out the kids and the dog and the bank account. He'd been running on the last of a small trust fund left to him, and had been hemorrhaging money through drink and sloth from nearly the moment his wife left until that day when he won at poker and found a pretty woman who used to give him excellent deep-tissue massage.

Mary gradually woke up just as twilight came on, and the stink of the man disgusted her, but as she moved away from him, his arm grasped her more tightly.

"Gimme kiss," he said. "Come on, baby. Just a little one."

She pressed her lips to his, and felt his hand going to her breasts. She let him continue, and soon he had unbuttoned her blouse and was rubbing through her bra before she reached back to undo it for him. In her mind she was younger and feeling the heat of fire within her as it rose. She knew she had power over men like this, and she wanted more from him than he'd be willing to give her if she resisted.

Soon his sweaty fingers teased her nipples as he began to grind himself against her. His tongue was all over her neck as if he could lick up all the sweat on her body, and she felt his hardness down there.

"I knew you wanted me," he whispered, his breath like warmth and bitterness together. "I knew you wanted me. All those times I was lyin' on your table. Practically naked. Just that little white towel you had. You ever see how it rose up sometimes when you worked on me? Ever notice? I bet you did. I told the guys that Jeannie wanted me like she wanted nobody else. You're that kind of girl, Jeannie. I knew it when I first saw you. You're so beautiful, baby. You are so beautiful. You may be almost my age, honey, but you look like a girl. That kind of girl. My kind of girl."

"I am," she murmured as his face moved from her breasts to her tight belly. "I am that kind of girl."

She no longer felt as if she were in her forties, but as if she truly were a girl again, and her stepfather was doing those things to her that brought out the wild animal inside.

The thing that turned her on, in a way that no other woman had ever been turned on.

He looked up at her, a sloppy grin on his face. "You like Daddy, don't you baby? You like what Daddy does to baby?"

"Oh," she gasped. "Yes. Yes." She pressed both hands against his scalp, pushing him farther down. She closed her eyes, and felt the shame course through her blood. She didn't hate him the way she hated them sometimes. She wanted him to feel how bad she was feeling. She wanted the pleasure of his understanding.

Then she let go of his scalp. She wrapped her legs around his face, and she leaned over just a bit, just enough to get her right hand on the small can opener she'd grabbed from the kitchen that morning, when they'd come in the house. When she told him she wanted another beer, and he'd grabbed a bottle for her, and she had popped it open and taken a sip. When he had been fumbling all over her, trying to make love then, only he was too wasted to even get his own fly down. And she had taken the can opener and put it aside, thinking she might use it. Thinking of its little sharp point.

Thinking of what kind of girl she was, and what things girls like her liked to do.

How she wanted to make sure he knew what it felt like to have someone jabbing you between the legs.

2

Mary took a shower in the enormous tub he had in a bathroom that was nearly as big as her own house. It felt good to wash the blood off, to be free of that awful feeling. As she passed the bedroom again, she went in, passing the body that lay sprawled on the bed, and reached into Nick's pants pockets for the key to his Cadillac.

Once in the car itself, she started it up and noticed that the gas gage was almost on empty, nearly at the same time the car's radio blared about the fires in the mountains, and that's when the idea came to her.

3

Two hours later, out on the ridge beyond the Belle-View Park where Nick Spitzer's house was, Mary Chilmark felt the dry gusts of wind at her back. The sweat on her body had evaporated, and she felt clean again.

It was a burning hot afternoon, and she smelled the distant fires across the freeway that had already jumped the San Bernardino Wash and had begun to head toward the railroad tracks off Baseline. The sky to the north was blackened from the smoke.

She knew the fire would never come this far—Caldwell was protected by too many natural fire breaks—unlike the San Bernardino foothills that just connected community after community right down to the 10 Freeway.

She set the gas can down and then went to gather dried sticks and tumbleweed. At the edge of an arroyo, she glanced over and saw the high razor-wire fences that surrounded Darden State.

She closed her eyes, sending a prayer to her son. Knowing that this would help him. Hoping that by her actions, she could free him again. Free him and find the one who had broken all his promises to her. The one who reminded her of every man she had ever been with.

The man who needed an even greater healing than her father had.

She blocked the bad memories of that place, and tried instead to remember where the entryways were, how the nurses looked when they walked into the building. Nobody would have a recent photo of her. The one in the newspapers made her look nearly blond, and although she had retained her youth in a way most women approaching fifty had not, and her figure now was better than at twenty-two, when the first few months of pregnancy were upon her, nobody at Darden State would even know who she was if she managed to get past the gate.

Well, maybe you, she thought. *Maybe you will know me. But if I see you, it'll be the last thing you see.*

Only one person from those days still worked there after all those years.

They would think she was just another nurse coming in, checking into her shift. She was a nurse, after all, and people could tell that about her when they saw her. She had that air of authority and compassion. She knew the words to speak that made people understand her position.

The Santa Ana winds had picked up. The sky from the north blackened.

And then she found the perfect property. It was surrounded by two acres of dry scrub brush and high yellow grass and a few dead orange trees at the center of this field.

She could taste the heat on the wind.

She poured two gallons of gasoline over the dry underbrush.

Then she set the fire.

By her calculation, it would spread, house to house, in Caldwell, and travel the fairly direct route right down the canyon. Might take the whole night to reach the flatlands, if the wind kept up. Might only take a few hours. It all depended on how the wind went and how dry the grasses were. She had seen on the news how the fires in the hill leapt acres, like a burning angel flying over rooftops. She had seen a car on the news where a couple had gotten trapped inside it while trying to drive away from it.

And that wind was hot and moving exactly where she wanted it to move.

The wind would carry it down the ridge, across the suburban community, and if luck was with her—as it always had been—it would bring the tongues of fire to Darden State.

She would find her child.

And his father.

PART THREE

CHAPTER TWENTY-TWO

1

Patients who had not had recent violent outbursts were allowed to mingle during certain activities—even the sexual psychopaths, so long as there was adequate supervision. In this respect, Darden State most resembled a maximum security prison. During the day, there might be classes and group therapy and even time in the game room playing video games or board games. In the library, patients were allowed to talk quietly, although if there was even the hint of someone getting out of control, the library would be shut for days at a time. Although budget cuts had helped lay off many of the guards and correctional officers, the canteen, during lunch and supper hours, always had at least six guards on hand in case of an outburst.

At 6 P.M., Doc Chilmark, still in leg restraints that kept him hobbling as he walked, was escorted by two guards to the canteen in Ward D.

His supper consisted of spaghetti with meatballs, a small salad, and a kaiser roll. There were no knives with dinner, but plastic spoons and forks sufficed for most of the patients.

Because he had remained docile, and because several correctional officers supervised the shifts of the canteen in the evening, upper body restraints had been removed from Doc as he sat at one of the long tables. A few other patients sat nearby, but few looked up at him, and no one seemed to want to sit near him, perhaps because one of the C.O.s sat next to Chilmark.

But Rob Fallon had noticed the new guy, and went over with his tray and sat down in front of him. "Rob," he said, nodding.

Doc Chilmark looked up at him, then back down to his plate. He dragged his fork through the spaghetti, rolling it up a bit before bringing it to his lips.

"I like welcoming new patients," Rob said. The C.O. next to Chilmark shot Rob a look, but said nothing. Rob ignored him.

"I don't like eating here after what I saw downstairs," Rob said.

Chilmark kept his eyes down. He reached for his small carton of milk and took a sip from it.

Rob leaned forward. "You got scars all over you."

Doc Chilmark finally looked at Rob Fallon. He said nothing. He kept chewing his food.

"I saw a ghost downstairs," Rob said. "Right under where we are."

2

After he was finished with supper, Doc Chilmark rose, with some assistance, and carried his tray over to the garbage can near the window into the canteen's kitchen. Rob Fallon walked with him. As he scraped the last of his food into the trash, Doc said, "I see ghosts all the time here. There are a lot of people who died here. They're like shadows."

"I know," Rob said. "The one I saw downstairs was a girl."

"Where's downstairs?" Chilmark asked, his voice so quiet that Rob barely heard him.

"Underneath here. There's a door. It leads underground," Rob said.

"I heard about it," Doc said, nodding. Rob had to lean over the table to hear him because his voice was so soft. "My mother told me. She was here once. She was down there when my soul came into her body. She told me the dead were everywhere there."

CHAPTER TWENTY-THREE

1

HRD—Human Remains Detection—was a special police canine department out of Riverside. Dahl and Laymon wasted no time calling them in, with the help of the Medical Examiner, to the house on Third Street that Mary Chilmark had been renting.

The detectives arrived with two dogs—one a black Labrador retriever, and the other a mutt that looked as if he were part border collie, part lab. Jane had expected the usual German Shepherds. "Cadaver dogs," the HRD guy said, "these guys are trained for this."

"I'm worried they might ruin evidence," Jane said, leaning down to give the mutt a scritch on the head.

"This one's named Scroungy," the officer said, grinning. "Best dog in the world. Training them's a weird experience, since you're burying body parts just for the puppies to go sniff out. But these two are the best. If there are bodies here, we'll find 'em."

"Let's check the backyard first," Jane said. "It's concrete."

"Ah," the officer said. "The classic burial."

2

In the backyard, the dogs sniffed around, and the one called Scroungy stayed close to the back door with his sniffs. The back lights were up bright, and Jane shone her flashlight around until she saw a series of discolorations—a slightly darker, smoother concrete area, when compared to the rest of the yard.

And Scroungy had begun scratching at the area not far from it.

"Let's get the jackhammers!" she shouted to Dahl, who was inside the house with the techs carefully gathering anything that might be evidence.

3

After nearly an hour of two of the guys cracking the surface with the jackhammers, Jane held up her hand to stop them. She crouched down along the crumbled concrete and brushed some of the debris away.

Embedded in it, not far beneath the surface: a human foot.

CHAPTER TWENTY-FOUR

1

In his office, Trey opened Mary Chilmark's files. They were made up of several pages of the usual state paperwork, the trial transcripts, the listings of the murders she'd committed. But those told him nothing. It was Brainard's notes he wanted. But the first set of notes he found—scribbled as if by an eleven-year-old on torn spiral notebook sheets—were those of Dr. Phillip Massey.

The man who helped get Mary's early release and who married her a few months later.

The man who had killed himself about five years before Mary and Doc Chilmark murdered the Flocks in their home.

2

The notes:

She is calm. She talks about her childhood. She

talks about how she was kept hungry when she was a little girl. She talks about how she got so thin by the age of eleven that her father began force-feeding her by putting his hands on each side of her jaw to open her mouth. How he made her milkshakes out of beef and tomato juice and forced her to drink them or she would receive punishment.

Her mind seems clear at this point. Three years here has done her good. I think she was living in a cloud of abuse as a child. Darden, and her therapy here, as well as the medications, have helped her examine these problems. She has begun to acknowledge the murders, but still feels that someone else did them. Someone who was near her all the time. I don't think this is a multiple personality problem. I think she clearly knows that she is responsible for those actions. She told me that she became aware of what she had done when she had tried to set fire to the beds. She felt as if she were a little girl again, trying to destroy evidence of some bad act she'd committed before her father had come in to punish her for it. When we go for walks on the grounds here and talk about how she handles pain, she said that she used to burn herself sometimes just to feel something. Or cut herself with scissors when she was a young girl. She expressed regret and horror at her own actions with regard to the murders, but she still feels disconnected from them at this stage.

Yet I cannot help thinking that Darden State may end up not being the right place for her. A halfway house, perhaps, with medication and ongoing therapy, might be better for her. She definitely has a moral sense of right or wrong, and talks about black-outs she had around the time of the murders.

There is one thing that still concerns me, though, and that is her interest in the occult. Not in some Judeo-Christian definition of it, but she believes that she has seen ghosts, particularly of those whom she killed. I suspect this is a manifestation of her conscience, and I hope that through our daily sessions I can bring her to a clearer understanding of her acts and her responsibilities with them.

She doesn't seem prone to depression at this point. Neither is she over medicated or lethargic. She has been developing a healthy attitude toward the world at large, and has been more than helpful with the other patients.

The patient is generally better adjusted than most of the other patients here, and given the overcrowding that has occurred with the shut-down of the A and B Wards while construction is ongoing, and the transitional state of the residence halls as well as D Ward, I recommend a course of therapy as well as an early release program.

3

Trey turned the notebook page over, and saw Dr. Robert Brainard's neat handwriting on two pieces of memo paper:

Dr. Massey,

I can't encourage you on this current course of action. We had an issue with Mary Chilmark with regard to her pregnancy. She will not tell me who the father of her child is, but she's aware that her pregnancy may help her gain early release into the general population. I know you've worked with her, and I understand your eagerness to see this patient back functioning in the world, but our responsibility to the community at large comes first. While she may be capable of living in the world, I recommend the low-security units, perhaps even in the residency housing outside the ward, but still on Darden's grounds.

Yes, I agree that her progress has been remarkable and her remorse convincing and authentic. We have all gotten to know Mary Chilmark well here, and she has many supporters among the staff.

I understand your professional commitment to her, and if you are willing to provide additional support and supervisory care for the duration of her pregnancy while she undergoes continued therapy and daily visits to Darden, I can sign off on this to some extent, but with caution. However, I do not think it advisable for you to take such a risk with a patient, no matter how that patient has recovered from past trauma and delusional behavior.

I want you to remember a patient named Shattuck in 1979, and how an early release impacted his life and the lives of the community to which he was released. Sometimes, a patient manages to fool us all. While I certainly feel that the years we've known Mary Chilmark mitigate against a reprisal of this kind of behavior, I can't help but feel that she should be in residency at least for another year of observation.

Sincerely,

R.B.

4

When Trey had finished going through the letters and notes in the file, he flipped through the pictures.

There was one of Mary Chilmark, then in her twenties, sitting on a chair in a lounge. It was an old scene, and her legs were crossed, her head thrown back slightly as if she owned the place. She had a cigarette in her right hand.

She was beautiful. She looked like the most glamorous young woman who had ever walked through Darden's doors. She reminded Trey of another patient who also had a great deal of beauty.

Beauty could be a weapon, particularly of the criminally insane. It could be used to seduce and then destroy what it had power over.

Strikingly, she looked like a feminine version of Doc Chilmark. The same waiflike face with large dark eyes. The dark hair. The slender arms.

But what Trey noticed most about this photograph was that it was not just another file photo taken of a patient. Whoever took this must have loved her. Whoever took this had caught her relaxing, and in her face—in those eyes—he saw the gleam of power.

She knew she owned whoever took the picture.

She knew she would be free of Darden State.

Where was this lounge? Things had changed so much a few years after Mary Chilmark had been a patient that Trey had no idea. He couldn't identify the wall behind her or the cigarette machines—which they no longer had at Darden and had never had in Trey's memory.

Had Massey taken the photo? Had he brought her into an employee lounge for the cigarette and snapped the picture? If so, why keep it in the files?

With Massey dead, there would be no answers to the questions.

Idly, Trey turned the photo over. Written on it: *Mary Chilmark, Darden State.*

Didn't seem particularly odd, but he was unsure why such a casual picture had been taken of her. It made her look like she was an employee on a cigarette break. There were a few other photos in there of her, more official shots, but none quite like this one.

The file on Chilmark was fairly thick and had the usual lists of her therapies, her meds, the letters from victims' families that always went to the board whenever the decision of early release was upon them.

Somewhere in there he saw a small scrap of paper that nearly fell out from between the rest of them.

He looked at it. He could barely read it.

He brought it right up to his face. It looked like chicken scratch across some printed words.

It had been torn from something else. Some kind of

paperwork. He rifled through the nearby papers, checking them, but none had been torn.

Trey closed the file, trying to forget that curious smile on Mary Chilmark's face in the photo of her in the lounge.

A smile that might've meant nothing at all.

Or might've meant everything.

He went through the papers, the transcripts from her trial that were briefly excerpted, and paused when he saw a page with a word crossed out in black magic marker. He flipped through the transcript: the name of the hospital where Mary Chilmark had murdered three patients was blacked out.

5

Less than fifteen minutes later, he stood outside Dr. Brainard's office. Diego, Brainard's assistant, had tried to dissuade him from standing vigil, but Trey kept Mary Chilmark's bulky file under his arm, and just waited outside the door.

After a minute, the door opened.

Brainard stood there. "I'm leaving in twenty minutes."

"Where did she commit those murders?" Trey asked.

He was sure he already had an answer.

CHAPTER TWENTY-FIVE

1

In Brainard's office the lights were dimmed, the blinds drawn. There was an end-of-the-day neatness to it. The wastebasket was empty. The top of his desk was in perfect order, and his computer had been shut down. The smell of a cinnamon-and-vanilla cachet hung in the air.

"You write in a note to Massey, in Mary's file, about having known her for years. Not the two years she was here in Ward D. But years. She was twenty-five years old when she committed the murders. You said she came to Darden fresh from nursing school. She was in Darden for just under two years, which was remarkable in and of itself," Trey said, following Dr. Brainard in. "I saw a picture of her. A photo someone left in the file. It looked like a nurse on a break, and not a patient."

Brainard went to the file cabinet, withdrew a key from his suit jacket pocket and unlocked the cabinet.

179

He opened it wide, thumbed through some files, and pulled a thick one out that had a rubber band around it.

When he turned around to face Trey again, Brainard wore an expression that Trey could only think of as bemused.

"It's sealed information," Dr. Brainard said. "But I'll let you see it. The state of California would crucify me professionally, Trey. If this got out, particularly with that news guy all over us, well, it would not be a pretty moment of Darden's past."

Trey took the files that Brainard had stacked on his desk. He opened the first one.

It was an employee file of the Darden State Hospital for Criminal Justice.

There was an old identification card with its clip still on it.

The photograph was of Mary Chilmark.

"In the 1980s, we were still transitioning," Brainard said, and sat on the edge of his desk. His voice was low and almost soft, as if he didn't like telling secrets. "Most of the wards were still the mentally ill. Ward C dealt with the mentally retarded, and only D had been used for the criminally insane verdicts. But state funding got cut, and eventually we had to release a lot of patients. It was about '84 when the funding came in to develop Darden as more for criminal justice than mental illness. She came to us as a nursing intern. In fact, I think she was in her last term—going to school during the day and working the night shift here. She was here two years before the incidents."

"The murders of three patients," Trey said, glancing up from Mary Chilmark's employee records.

"Yes."

"The state wanted her employment records sealed?"

"Sure. What are you, a Boy Scout? Scandals happen in hospitals. Particularly ones like this. Not often. Maybe every thirty years. Somebody bungles. Hospitals don't just run on purity and light. Something happens. It was a sensitive point, you've got to understand that. Funding was coming in. It was simply to keep trouble from happening. When a hospital like Darden transitions, nobody wants trouble. You think this information would help the police in their investigation?"

Trey thought for a moment. "I don't know. Maybe it would. Maybe it wouldn't."

"It wouldn't. She was a good nurse. Very young. Even gifted. I suppose that's why we were all protective of her. The patients loved her. But the PTS she sustained, and her father's abuse all those years, and then, if she was at all to be believed, when the male patient raped her . . ."

"He raped her? Do we know this for a fact?"

"No. There's no way to know it. It was simply her word at the time, after she murdered him. But he had been a sexual deviant, per the state code at the time."

Trey closed the folder. "Is there anything else that needs to be known about Chilmark?"

"She saved another nurse's life. We all were witness to it. A patient was coming after the other girl, and Mary put herself in harm's way, getting stabbed twice in the shoulder. But the other girl—another young nurse—would've been killed."

"The way Mary Chilmark kills," Trey said, "she probably killed the patient who attacked."

Dr. Brainard said nothing in reply. He stood up again and went to his office door. "If we're finished here," he said, opening the door.

The light from the hallway seemed too bright as Trey rose and set the file back on Brainard's desk.

As Trey went out into the hall, Dr. Hannafin's assistant, Lara, called out to him, "Hannafin wants to grab you, if she can."

"Why not?" Trey asked, and leaned against the reception counter. "Day I'm having, I'm never getting home."

2

"You wanted to see me?" Trey asked after tapping lightly on the door. When he tapped, the door slid open slightly. As soon as Hannafin saw him, she swiveled around her chair and got up and came toward him as if she were in a rush. "He's been acting out some more. I want you to come with me."

She brushed past him out the door, and he stared at her a second before he began following her out into the corridor.

3

In the elevator down to the first floor of Ward D, he said, "I'm probably breaking a confidence, but his mother was a nurse here."

Hannafin glanced up at him—she'd been staring at her feet waiting for the elevator to move between floors. "Mary Chilmark was here?"

"Darden was transitioning between being a hospital with both the mentally ill and the criminally insane, to being what it is now. She murdered patients here."

She shook her head slightly. "Nothing surprises me anymore. Well, that doesn't really help us with the son right now. Look. He wants you there when I talk to him. For some reason, he's attached to you. I can't tell if this is good or bad—his feeling so comfortable with you."

"Probably bad," Trey said. "Maybe I shouldn't go."

"No, it's good for the most part. There's something about you that makes him relax." She looked straight ahead at the closed elevator doors as she said this.

"Maybe it's the straitjacket," Trey said.

She ignored his comment. "Do you know where this rumor about ghosts came from?"

"Ghosts?"

"He started to get violent and screamed about the shadows of the dead crawling on him," she said. "Right after he ate. Nobody knows what brought it on."

"He started screaming? Wow. He was calm when I saw him earlier. Maybe it was Fallon."

"Why him?"

"When we found him in the underground, he said he saw ghosts. Maybe he's been talking this up on the ward. That's the only thing I can guess."

"Ugh," she said. "That underground. I don't know why they don't just seal it up."

The elevator doors opened. They stepped out, went through the security check, and on down to Program 28.

4

"He let them out," Doc Chilmark said. In the comfort of his straitjacket, he leaned back on his cot and looked up at the ceiling rather than at Trey, Hannafin, or Atkins, who stood near the door to Chilmark's room.

"Doc, there really are no ghosts down there," Susan Hannafin said. "Let's talk about the anxiety you're experiencing. Are you managing to rest at all?"

"No. I can't remember sleeping. I feel like I've been up for a week."

Then Doc twisted his head around to look over at Trey. "I'm glad you're here."

"Why's that?"

"You keep them away."

"Who?"

"The shadows," Doc said. "They live underground here. And they come out now because people have been opening the door for them. There must be a lot of them down there."

Susan shot a glance at Trey that seemed to suggest: *Just let him talk.*

"I heard one of them when I was eating tonight. If you call that food. I heard this little girl."

Trey remembered Rob Fallon claiming there was a girl ghost, and filed this away to mention it to Hannafin later on.

"I heard her. She's trapped down there. Others are trapped there, too. But they're leaking out now. At night they come out and change shapes and get through doorways," Doc said fairly matter-of-factly. "The world changes at night in the dark. That's why they become night fears. They move through keyholes. They take people over. I'm not safe here." He had never once let his gaze wander from Trey's face. It was as if the only thing in the room he could look at was Trey.

Afterward, in the hallway, walking swiftly back down the ward, Susan Hannafin said, "He trusts you at this point. That's good. I don't want you to do the police's bidding too much with this. He's at a very delicate point. Even though he's a prisoner here, we can't ever forget his mental state and his health needs, Trey. Let's leave the lights on for him tonight. No point in him staying up all night after lights out. His prescription should start kicking in tonight—when the nurses do the ten o'clock meds, he'll get some Cambex to help him sleep through the night, but we'll keep the lights on in his room anyway. If the Cambex doesn't work immediately, I want him to feel safe above all else."

"Sounds good," Trey said. "Let's hope Fallon hasn't infected everybody on Ward D with the ghost story."

5

Rob Fallon had already been telling others about the ghost he'd seen beneath Darden State, and the word got around further. When Trey took off for the night, Rita Paulsen, who was working double shifts that week, stopped to tell him, "This is going to be one of those nights—a full moon, ghost stories, and one of the psych techs already has been pretending he heard a ghost, too."

It was the way of the wards at Darden. Once a rumor started among the patient population, it became like a contagion. Trey figured that by the next morning, every single patient on the first floor, particularly of Ward D, would be complaining that a ghost had come into their rooms through the vents.

Once he reached the parking lot, sitting in his car, he took a deep breath, then let it all out. He knew he'd have to do a good two- to three-mile jog that evening once the kids were in bed, just to blow off the steam of the day.

On his way home, he stopped in the a bookstore in the State Street Mall in Redlands and picked up a copy of Dr. Susan Hannafin's book.

Chapter Twenty-six

In his room, wrapped in the warmth of his straitjacket after having it taken off when he needed to use the toilet, Doc Chilmark curled up in a ball, not on top of his cot, but just beneath it. He tried to pretend that it was his cage. He tried to pretend, squeezing his eyes shut as hard as he could make them, that he was back at home with Mary. Feeling her kisses on the back of his neck before she went to her own bedroom.

But instead he remembered things that frightened him.

He remembered the men who regularly came into the house, the ones who took off all their clothes and lay down on the table.

All the filthy men who touched her. She was too pure for them. But they touched her anyway.

All of them needed healing, and after they had gone, each one leaving money on the table, Mary had come to him and held him and told him that it was all right. That time was not the enemy. "All men are like that except you," she murmured to him, holding him tight, drawing him from his cage, out onto the floor. His head against her breasts, his arms about her waist. "They all need healing. Women, too. Everybody has the disease in them. But you have the cure for it. You and I both, Doc."

Doc lay in the room in Program 28 and began crying. He missed her touch too much. He didn't know why she hadn't come for him yet. She always had come for him in the past, even after she'd left him as a boy with Cooper Fenn. Even after Dr. Massey had died. She'd come for him, no matter what was keeping her back.

He didn't think he could live without her.

He fought the feelings of sleep, though he was exhausted.

Something made a noise in his room. He opened his eyes, looking out from under the bed.

Something was there.

Even with the lights on.

The shadows were coming.

Crawling.

Night fears on their way.

Maybe just outside the door.

Out in the dark of the hallway.

He glanced over at the grate just the other side of cot.

What if they were down there, trying to come up?

For just a second, he was sure he heard the voice of a little girl say something.

He closed his eyes and tried to blot out any sound he heard.

Please come soon. Please, Mary. Don't leave me here. You promised you'd never leave.

CHAPTER TWENTY-SEVEN

1

The first call came for Trey Campbell at eleven o'clock that night. It was Jane Laymon. He'd tried to reach her earlier, but had to leave message after message for her. He hadn't expected to hear from her again until morning.

Trey had been reading Dr. Susan Hannafin's book, *The Killer Instinct: Inside the Minds of Seven Psychopathic Murderers,* lying in bed with the covers half on and half off, while Carly did her yoga over near the French doors that led to the courtyard. He'd just read beyond the introduction when his cell phone light began blinking—he barely noticed it at first, and then wanted to ignore it.

He took off his glasses, picked up the phone, and popped it open. "Hello?"

"Trey. Got a minute?"

Trey sat up, setting the book down. He got out of bed, slipped his briefs on, and made an understood hand signal to Carly, who got out of her stretching position and stood up, watching him. He covered the phone for a second. "It's Jane," he said.

"I figured," Carly said.

Trey walked past her to the bedroom door, went out into the hallway, and took the phone with him out the front door. He sat on the low step. It was a peaceful night, although the vague scent of smoke from distant fires was in the air. "Jane? All right."

"We found more bodies."

"In her house?"

"Beneath it. I should've noticed it the first time I went out back. The whole backyard is concrete, but there's a little color difference near the back door. That's where she must've repaired the concrete and then re-set it—after burying her victims. Two of the victims were buried shallow. I'd guess about eight inches down, under just about two inches of concrete."

Trey swore under his breath.

"Yeah, we got cadaver dogs out, and when they seemed to locate a spot near the back door, we got some jackhammers in and went at it. First time I've ever seen this kind of work. Blood Mary was quite the handywoman. Her landlady told me she fixed things all the time. But there's one other thing, Trey. She lived within spitting distance of Darden."

"You're kidding."

"Nope. And get this: She had him sleeping in a dog crate. Her son. Handcuffs, ropes, all kinds of restraints."

"Straitjacket?"

"Yep. She had lots of stuff right out of a medical catalog. Looked really S&M to me. I'm assuming you figured out the nature of their relationship?"

"Incest. Abuse. I wish none of this surprised me," he said. "She's in Caldwell?"

"Yep. If I walk to the end of her block, and go to the back of the houses there, I can practically wave to the guards at Darden. You know how the town grows out into the foothills? Her neighborhood's up there. And I bet she spent a lot of time looking at Darden. Why would she do that?"

"Because she worked as a nurse at Darden. The three patients she killed as a nurse were patients at Darden."

Jane remained silent for a few seconds. "What?"

"I saw the state records of her employment. Earlier. I just didn't think it would matter. I didn't think she'd be living up on some hillside watching the place. Jane, I think she's obsessed with Darden State."

"She was a fucking nurse at Darden?" Jane said as if she hadn't heard it right. "Does that happen much?"

Trey chuckled. "Okay, it's not funny. I'm just tired. It happens now and then. Sometimes the person who gets hired to work at Darden comes with a full set of serious psych issues themselves. I've certainly seen it happen. Usually, it's the psychologists." He chuckled again, and then apologized for being a little punchy. "In fact, her obsession with Darden might be entirely normal, given everything else. She works there, she murders patients, she's put in Ward D, she gets pregnant by someone there, she gets out. Makes some sense if the major events of her adult life—being that

191

dramatic—happened there. It becomes her little pond to watch."

"Who's the candidate for daddy?"

"You mean to Doc? No idea. Rumors fly. Most likely it was Massey."

"And he's dead now."

"That definitely was suicide?"

"Yep," Jane said. "No question. Here's what we have so far. She befriended a woman named Patty Mullen. Patty was having money troubles, so she needed a roommate, and Bloody Mary stepped right in, but left her son with Cooper Fenn for a bit. Then Mary killed Patty—possibly. We can't quite track down who Patty Mullen was. We haven't found a body yet, but I suspect we will."

"Jane, I know that name. Patty Mullen," Trey said. "Christ, I think she used to work at Darden, too. I don't know everybody, particularly in the other wards. But that name is too familiar."

"Can you check on that for me?"

"Tomorrow, sure," he said. "But I may be wrong. Maybe it just sounds familiar. God, maybe I'm just getting paranoid about Bloody Mary."

"It would certainly fit if she worked at Darden. And it would make sense for her to live so close to work," Jane said. "My guess is that Mary, who called herself Jean, murdered Mullen right away. Set up the massage practice to pay bills, and now and then felt she had to kill a client or two. There's more stuff in the house— indications that Doc Chilmark had a hellish life with his mother. I still can't quite figure out the timing on this."

Trey said the first thing that came to his mind. "Poetic justice."

"Trey?"

"It's the thing Brainard said. It's why Mary was in Darden State in the '80s. She cuts off a guy's balls and stuffs them in his mouth because she claimed he tried to force himself on her that way. She and Doc kill Diane Flock and her husband—and their unborn baby—for some reason we haven't figured out yet. And now Doc is in the house where he was conceived."

"His father's house," Jane said.

"Right. Right. I know there's something in this that we're not noticing."

Jane's voice changed when she spoke next. It seemed to come out as almost a cough. "The baby," she said.

"What baby?"

"We never found the unborn baby at the Flocks. Diane Flock was only six months along, so the baby is definitely dead. They cut Diane Flock open, kill the baby in the process, take it. For what? She's kept it, Trey. Maybe she hid it someplace."

"Why in God's name would she do that?"

"We can safely assume she's operating on a different set of rules than most of us," Jane said. "At this point, I think she's getting creative."

2

After the call, Trey had trouble going to sleep, so he kissed Carly goodnight and took his book out to the living room. He switched on the lamp by the couch, plopped down in it and began flipping pages. But he couldn't focus on Dr. Hannafin's tales of Ward D, or her past work at Camarillo. He stared out the windows onto the courtyard and kept thinking of Doc Chilmark. Not as a nineteen-year-old, but as a little boy in a crate. Tied up. Treated, at best, like a dog.

He tried to imagine what Doc's mother must've been like. A woman who, through her own psychosis, had nurtured her son to the point where he could not distinguish between reality and fantasy. Where he had become his mother's perfect lover. Perfect confidante. It was almost as if she had bred him in order to have a second set of hands to do her dirty work. She'd raised and trained a psychopath in her image.

To the point where he did not feel pain at the suffering of others.

He did not feel remorse at the torture and murder of a woman who was six months pregnant.

Trey closed his eyes, remembering the thin scars on Doc's face.

Bloody Mary had burned him. She had abused him. She had . . .

Trey opened his eyes. He didn't like to think about it.

Jane had told him that the crime scene in the Flocks' house had been set up almost as a makeshift operating room.

Doc had performed the surgery. He was a healer. He was a doctor, at least in his mind. Doc had been raised to believe he had this power, and for some reason he had decided to use it on Diane Flock.

Mary had been there. She was a trained nurse. She

probably even told him exactly how to cut Diane Flock open. How to kill the unborn child. And then, how to tear open Diane's husband when he intruded on the scene.

How could a woman trained to help the sick do what she did?

Finally, as these thoughts roiled around Trey's mind, he fell asleep on the couch dreaming of psychopaths and bloodshed, only to be awakened several hours later by another call on his cell phone.

CHAPTER TWENTY-EIGHT

1

The fire that Mary Chilmark had set earlier in the evening had begun slowly. The underbrush burned gradually, steadily, along the overgrown side yard of the house she'd chosen, and she had gone some distance away from it to watch. After several hours, it had finally picked up speed as the hot wind began shifting again. By that time, she'd gone back to the house by the golf course, where the body of Nick Spitzer lay in the bedroom on the second floor. She needed a few hours' rest before she went down to Darden State to find her son.

She had left a small bag in the Cadillac, and checked for it before entering the house.

She opened the bag and gazed down at what was in it.

For a moment, she remembered the first time she'd felt her son growing inside her.

2

The fire began to rise up sometime after midnight, climbing the house, which burned quickly. Inside, a family had to get out fast, for the smoke alarms hadn't worked, and if it hadn't been for the pet German shepherd barking, there was a chance that no one inside would be saved. The owner of the house turned on the sprinkler system and began spraying the roof of the house to try to protect it, but it was far too late. If he were to describe how the fire moved, he would say that it was like a demon from hell, leaping from his rooftop to the house next door, while all around his backyard became a wall of fire.

It moved quickly through the community, with palm trees bursting into flame along the roadway. Because new growth had come up after a fire in the wash several years before, the flames found new fuel, and the fire department was called, but firefighters were already up on a mountain on the opposite side of the valley, many miles away, so it took more time than usual for the trucks to come out. Helicopters were the first to get there, but they were few and far between because of the fires in the distant mountains, which had been raging for several days.

Not more than four miles away from where Mary Chilmark had spent the past five years in a rental house, under which she'd buried Patty Mullen, a man named Wilcox, and another man named Harrison, the fires raced along the canyon, palm trees like giant torches lighting up the night sky in Caldwell, California.

The dry winds met the flames, causing them to flare up to the sky.

Trey Campbell, who lived more than twenty miles away in Redlands, received his second call at 4:30 A.M.

This time, it was from Jim Anderson.

Chapter Twenty-nine

1

Trey left his house at five A.M., after a quick shower and some cold coffee left over from the previous day. He felt a little bleary-eyed, but something about the emergency got his adrenaline pumping.

On the cell phone as he drove along the streets of Redlands, heading out to the freeway, he asked Jim, "What's the scoop from Olsen?"

Jim Anderson, on the line, said, "Somebody was supposed to call for more buses. We're anticipating six hours of loading and cleanup."

"What's the guesstimate for the fire?"

"Might be as long as fourteen hours if it doesn't jump the wash. If it jumps the wash and the drainage ditch out at the boulevard, we're looking at eight. You almost here?"

"Almost," Trey said.

"You as sleepy as me?"

"Sleepier."

"Marcus Weirdo is here," Jim said, referring to one of the clinical directors, who had a more-than-slight problem with cocaine addiction. His real name was Mark Weir, and whenever any major emergency happened—a near riot, a lockdown, or even misplaced files that the state needed fast, the guy went into coke-head overdrive. Although Weir had spent time in rehab, it obviously had not worked, and Trey could just imagine how things were going with trying to keep the patients calm and in some semblance of order while Weir and others were cracking up in the face of an emergency.

"I don't get it, did the fire jump over the freeway?" Trey asked, as he came around the curve off Oleander and turned onto the aptly named Brown Industrial Road, a short cut over to Caldwell and the hospital.

"Not that fire from San Berdoo," Jim said. "This is a new one. Started up in the hills in Caldwell, some streets are toast now. It's skipping houses now and then. You know, it's like the hammer of hell coming down up there. Once you get on the boulevard, you'll see it."

Just as Trey closed the cell phone and made a few zig-zag turns, he saw the wall of flame up in the canyon. It was both magnificent and terrifying. "Holy shit," he said.

He pulled the car over for a second and just looked at it.

It was as if the canyon would be gone soon. Up beyond it lay the town of Caldwell. On the other hillside, about two miles away from where Trey had stopped, Darden State.

2

The sky had grown darker than night, covered by billowing clouds of black and gray smoke. The air definitely was warmer as he drove up the side streets to the main boulevard to Darden.

He thought he heard the shouts of people nearby—and then he saw pedestrians out on the street, pointing to the hills. Trey looked up quickly, just in time to see a fireball explode in the darkness. Then another, up on the burning hill.

Traffic on Jackman Boulevard, the main road that passed by Darden, was heavy as people were getting out of Caldwell and its surrounding areas. Lines of cars blocked the road, all of them with belongings tied to the roof or bulging from overstuffed trunks that had been tied with ropes. There was no sound of sirens at all. Trey assumed that was because it was unnecessary. The firefighters were probably up in the hills, doing what they could to contain the conflagration.

Trey imagined most of the houses on three of the hills and the nearby arroyo were gone.

Parking in the Darden lot, he glanced back at the fire up on the hillside.

"Shit," one of the nurses said to another woman, as she passed him on her way in to work. "I can't fucking believe I have to come in here four hours after I just signed off shift."

One of the senior psych techs from Ward C passed by, a man in his fifties named Dave Sledd. When Trey asked him about his house up in the canyon, Sledd said, "We barely had twenty minutes to get out of there. We grabbed the kids, the wedding pictures, and the cat, and just ran out. My wife had cinder burns on her shirt."

"God," Trey said. "I'm sorry."

"Hey, if I think about it too much, I'm gonna start crying," the psych tech said, a crooked grin on his face that looked more grim than jovial. He sighed. "We got insurance. It'll just be a problem for a while. My wife and girls are down at her sister's in Corona at this point. I can't believe that somebody started that thing. With all the fires over on the mountains, you'd think these firebugs would get a clue. Sons-of-bitches. Almost six hundred thousand acres up in the mountains have gone. Now this, over here. There must be at least seventy or eighty homes gone already, minimum. Including mine. And now look at us, Trey. We're gonna somehow get more than a thousand psychos and sociopaths out of these buildings in the next five hours? You think? What a day we're heading into."

3

"Where are the buses?" Trey asked the security guards at the front.

"Somebody fucked up," one of them said. "They were supposed to get them from Riverside, but Riverside already had sent some over to San Bernardino and Pomona because of the fires over there. A lot of hospitals are in evacuation mode right now. We're just the latest one. This is happening all over—four fires off the freeway. We're number five."

"When do we get ours?"

The other guard chuckled. "I suggested they try the schools. Get school buses. Get our guys in restraints and just move 'em out."

The hallways were pandemonium—and not any of the patients were out of their rooms. It was all administrators and nurses and psych techs. Some of the psychologists had come in to help calm patients, but Trey began to feel that they'd be better off working with the administration. Nobody wanted to do what had to be done here. Trey had seen this kind of mess more than once, each time with a different administration. Nobody really planned for the big emergencies, and Trey wondered how they were going to get all the patients out, and even when they did, where to?

He pressed his way between staff—several of them people he'd never seen before in all his years at the job—and as he passed the patients' rooms, he saw most of them up and getting ready to move out. Just standing at their doors, staring out through the small windows into the hallway.

He met up with Jim Anderson on Ward D, and Anderson took him through the checklist that "Marcus Weirdo" had set up. They went room to room—Susan Hannafin was already in, also going into each room to speak with the patients. "It's ballsy of her," Jim said. "She's operating on caffeine as far as I can tell. But she's doing the job none of the other doctors seem to want to do."

"She's good," Trey said. "Okay, let's go through this bogus checklist and make sure our ward's all set. How's Program 28?"

"In its own lockdown for now. That was Brainard's call."

"He's here already?"

"Yeah, somewhere. But he called early and told Hannafin and all the directors to close down four of the programs off the wards because they could wait until the wards had gotten their all-clears. Everybody's in a rush to get this show on the road. I say burn the place down." Jim guffawed. "Okay, I'm just going nuts 'cause of lack of sleep. I think I got about four good hours in at the most."

"I don't think I even got three," Trey said.

"So we got our marching orders, and most of the wards are in good shape patient-wise, but not so good with staff. Surprise, surprise. We get D all hooked up, roll 'em out like a cattle drive, and then maybe we're home free."

"Makes sense," Trey said. "Okay, well, where do we start?"

"I guess we use the emergency drill procedures, and hope for the best." Jim grinned, slapping Trey's arm lightly with the clipboard.

"More coffee, first," Trey said.

CHAPTER THIRTY

1

Outside, the fire burned along the canyons and arroyos. The morning sky was black with smoke, heavy with the smell of burning mesquite and sage and rubber and fresh wood and dried grass and gasoline from cars that had been blasted with flames. The fire department had helicopters flying overhead to bring water to part of the canyon that could not otherwise be reached, but these only arrived once every hour or so because they were being used as well with the fires up in the San Bernardino mountains to the north.

The buses rolled in to the Darden State grounds. Boxes of files were being transferred into SUVs that were lined up along the residency halls; the psychiatrist and psychologist parking lots were full as the professionals came in to save their computers and work and take out the family pictures from their offices. The psych techs had been recruited to stand alongside the patients, many of them in leg hobbles and wrist restraints, waiting to board one of the buses. Nurses worked alongside some of the patients in wheelchairs or those needing special assistance, and with the exception of the lockdown in Ward D, things on the outside of the hospital looked as if they were moving well toward evacuation of the buildings at Darden State. Every single employee of Darden State—from the janitors to the work crew to the techs and orderlies and guards—were called in to assist with the evacuation.

No one with an official identification card was refused admittance, although the security guard who checked at the front gate did not always notice the expiration date, nor were most of them scanned into the system as would be the normal procedure.

Mary Chilmark walked up the sidewalk to the guard who sat in his black and white SUV at the gate, near the now-closed sentry area. She showed her I.D., and though it was the identification badge of a woman named Patty Mullen who had not worked at Darden State in nearly five years, the guard waved her through, along with several other staff members from various departments—from the night shift, from the three A.M. swing shift from the day shifts—many of whom had never seen one another before, who had parked out on the street and walked up to the entry to the grounds.

In Mary Chilmark's hand was a small grocery bag. If anyone asked her, she would tell them it had her uniform in it. As nonsensical as that might seem for a woman coming to the grounds of a hospital threatened by fire, she felt that it would have to do, because if she told them what she had in the bag, they would most likely stop her.

But she'd been waiting a long time for this.

She had spent years planning her return to Darden State.

How she'd perform the operation that would be her and her son's greatest work.

And it moved the way she had dreamed it would. It moved with a rush of excitement within her, as she began to see the world again as one that had a clear and urgent purpose. Her mind felt revived by the smoke in the air and the hushed yet excited talk among those who were headed into the facility.

She floated above all of them—she was the wind itself, driven to this place, this present moment, and her son, waiting for her, probably watching for her to come and protect him from the fears that crawled in the dark.

And her boy's father there, too.

The one who had made her a promise so many years ago, broken but not discarded.

The promise lived in her heart.

He would feel what she had felt.

He would come to understand it.

2

There was an old bungalow-style building behind the residency hall, and within it a gardener's toolroom. It was kept locked at all times because of the potential for patients to find weapons—known in the hospital parlance as "sharps." Mary Chilmark had a set of keys that her late husband, Dr. Massey, had in his possession at his death. In fact, she had keys to nearly every building in Darden State because her late husband had gathered them for her one by one over the years they were together. Whenever he had wanted to touch her, he had to bring her a key. It was a game they played, and it made their love life exciting. They played so many games together, and she missed him. He had played games with their son, too, not the naughty kind, but the ones that involved the cage. He had been the only man who had ever understood what went on in her mind, and she had loved him for it. She had loved him, and had been truly bereft after he had the accident in which he died.

After he had taken a scalpel to his own wrists in a bath.

It was a night when she was with her son, holding him to chase away the fears.

She had kept the keys, labeling each one with a code so she would know where it fit. Where the secret places were at the hospital. Where she would find what she needed.

It had been to this very tool room—just a small room that had been used for storage for years—that she and her various lovers might go when she was young and in love with a handful of doctors at the hospital.

3

Inside the toolroom, she bypassed the shears and the pitchforks in favor of a large metal cabinet, full of spades and trowels and small pots for plants. The cabinet was not one she had ever seen before, but it didn't surprise her that it was there.

She slipped her fingers behind it, and drew the cabinet back from the wall. Slowly, she pulled the cabinet, then shoved it a bit to the left and outward.

Behind it was a short wide doorway, not more than four feet high, shut tight and padlocked.

But she had more keys, and after she tried several of them, one fit—the padlock clicked and opened.

She drew the door open.

A warm gust of mildewed air came back to her.

She crouched down, feeling with her hand along the wall within the room. When she found a switch, she flicked it up.

A pale blue light flickered on and then went out. When she toggled the switch again, it came up, and she saw the slender stairs downward into the uppermost level of the hospital's underground.

It was the place where she had made love to her son's father for the first time. Down in the secret spaces where only certain personnel had access.

Down among the night cages, where he had lain her back on the table, and she had wrapped her legs around him and given herself to him in a way she never had for any man before.

Risen to meet his thrusts, all the while feeling the shadows of the dead around them and knowing that above them in the world of light, the hospital continued.

Knowing that the promise he made to her was real and would last forever.

4

Mary Chilmark stepped down into the blue-lit stairwell at six A.M.

CHAPTER THIRTY-ONE

1

By seven A.M. the first several prison buses from Chino had come out, and then the loading up of the wards began. The best that anyone could do was house the patients down in Riverside, at the Parkside Community Hospital in a new wing that hadn't yet been filled. Ward D—the maximum-security ward—would have to be shipped out to L.A. County and their prison hospital that was new and not yet filled. So Ward D would go last, and probably wouldn't get the final patients out until about eleven.

Lance Victor got through with his cameraman, Carl, and was in the administration director's face, having hauled ass out of the hotel over in San Bernardino to get an "on-the-scene report as the Darden State Hospital for Criminal Justice attempts to evacuate its patients within three hours before a raging fire descends from the hills." When Trey passed by, Lance sidled up to him and said, "I just want some footage of the wards."

"They're nearly empty," Trey said. "What good's that gonna do you?"

"Please," Lance said. "You won't notice Carl or me."

"Just you," the security guard behind them said. "Not both of you. If you want to go get some pictures for your show, only one of you goes through."

"Yikes," Jim laughed. "Don't let either of them in. This place is a circus already."

After nearly all the wards were clear, with only Program 28 left to escort out, the worst thing happened.

Somewhere between the nurses running around with hypodermic needles full of tranquilizers, psych techs having to hold back patients who had begun getting the idea that this could turn into a free-for-all, and the administration's complete lack of understanding that they had a city full of psychopaths who, if their meds weren't quite kicking in, would be happy to tear out some eyeballs and rip some throats just because they got excited by doing it, an alarm pen sounded from one end of the nearly empty ward. Every staff member on Ward D had an alarm pen. Once the button at the top of the pen was punched, a brief clanging alarm sounded for about three seconds, followed by a strobe effect of lights along the corridor, leading right to the person who had set off the alarm.

And this meant, in a matter of five minutes, a lockdown, unless it could be determined that none was necessary.

"Jeez Louise," Jim said. "Lance Victor's gonna love this."

"At least the ward's pretty clear," Trey said.

The strobe lights came up on the ceiling, moving like lightning along the corridor. Trey, Jim, and two of the guards began walking swiftly past the nurses and other staffers going the opposite direction, all of whom seemed to have begun moving in slow motion in front of them. As they went farther down the corridor, the ward seemed empty of all but a few stragglers from among the staff.

PART FOUR

CHAPTER THIRTY-TWO

Jane Laymon tried to call Trey on his cell phone. When that didn't work, she attempted to reach him through the main switchboard at Darden, but she still couldn't get through.

When she'd been called back up to the rented house on Third Street in Caldwell—the techs felt they had to make sure that the place had a last going-over, in case the fire spread up toward that end of the hillside—she had sifted through the evidence and found a detailed layout of Darden State.

And worse, a layout of the basement level of the hospital with rooms marked: night cage. Several of them.

Another area—an upper floor of Ward D—was marked with just the words: his office.

With traffic backed up on the hillside and plumes of darkness coughing from the burning canyon, Jane drove alone down toward Darden State, determined to find out if Bloody Mary might be traced right back to the place where she had worked, where she had met her husband, and where her son was being held.

CHAPTER THIRTY-THREE

1

When Trey rounded the first hallway in Ward D, he saw something near the elevators. The strobes continued to flash on and off, and what he found inside the elevator, its doors open wide, nearly made him drop to his knees and scream.

Lara, Susan Hannafin's assistant, lay facedown on the floor in a pool of blood.

In her hand, she still clutched the alarm pen that she'd punched to set off the warning.

Trey crouched down to feel her pulse.

She was gone. He touched the back of her neck. Right at the base of her skull, someone had jabbed a knife of some kind into her.

Jesus. Lara. Jesus, he thought.

"Jim! Hurry up!" he called. Jim Anderson came up behind him, cursing under his breath when he saw the dead woman.

221

2

Down several hundred feet and to the right, at the entrance to Program 28, Mary Chilmark, still clutching her grocery bag in one hand, had the other pressed into Dr. Robert Brainard's spine.

Brainard waved them past the guards and said, "We're going to escort Chilmark to a special transport. I'll send someone else down for the others."

Floyd Nelson grinned. "You're gonna need a guard with you, Dr. Brainard. You see those strobes?" He pointed back down the hallway. "I think we're gonna be in lockdown any minute, and the ward's not even clear yet. Hope nothing too awful's going on."

"It's nothing," Brainard said rather stiffly. "Someone accidently pulled it."

"Accidents happen," Mary Chilmark said, smiling slightly.

"Well, at least let me escort the two of you," Floyd said.

"Yes," she said. "That's a good idea." Then, as if it needed to be added, she said, "I'm a nurse from San Pascal General. We'll have a special place for him over there."

"Lucky him," Floyd said, and then accompanied the two of them down the corridor to Doc Chilmark's room. He unlocked the door, and stepped inside before the others.

Doc got up out of bed, standing before the guard. "Okay, Mr. Chilmark," Floyd said. "It's time to move on."

But at the door on the way out, Mary Chilmark took

the long ice pick she had in her hand, and swiftly jabbed it into Floyd Nelson's ribs, using all her strength.

Brainard grabbed her arm, but she pulled the pick out, and pressed it against the hand that held her, piercing the skin until Brainard let go.

Doc Chilmark was already on Dr. Brainard, using all his force to push the man down to the floor, ramming the doctor's head twice against the wall as he did so.

After he'd subdued Brainard, Doc went to get the gun and the tazer from Floyd Nelson's body.

3

Trey and Jim took the walkie-talkies off two guards who went running back down the hall to get some reinforcements. The strobe lights kept flashing, and Trey decided for the safety of others it would be better not to shut them down. "You go check out 28," Trey said. "Get Floyd and Atkins, and anyone else you can find. I'm going upstairs."

He took the stairs two at a time up to the second floor to check the psychiatrist offices where Lara had come down. It didn't seem likely someone had gotten her on D, given that the ward at floor level was in pretty good shape.

When he came out of the stairwell into the series of offices, he saw Dr. Hannafin standing at the elevator, trying to get her cell phone to work. Beside her were several boxes full of files.

She glanced over at him. "What the hell happened to you?"

He looked at his hands—covered in blood. "How long have you been up here?" he said.

"What?"

"The strobe's going off downstairs," he said. "Lara's dead. Someone killed her. Someone got on the elevator and went down from here, with her in it."

"Lara? Dead?" Hannafin gave him a puzzled look. "What the hell is going on? Are you bleeding?"

"A patient is out. Someone. Running amok. Has a knife, maybe."

"Christ," Hannafin said. "I saw her—Lara—ten minutes ago. She and Robert got on the elevator."

"Dr. Brainard? Just them? Anyone else?"

Dr. Hannafin squinted at Trey as if trying to remember something. "Somebody else. A woman."

"A patient?"

"No," Hannafin said. "I don't know who. She looked like she was staff. I thought . . . I thought she was helping." Then, "Jesus, Lara's *dead?*"

Trey heard a crackle from the walkie-talkie. He lifted it up and pressed the button. "Jim? What's up?"

"In the canteen," Jim said, his voice a whisper. "I see Brainard. He's got some people with him. God, Lance Victor's there with his camera. But one of them . . . one looks like Chilmark. What the hell does Brainard have him in the canteen for? Hang on . . . hang on . . ."

"Jim, is there a woman with them? Jim?" Trey asked. No answer. Just the crackle of static on the line. "Jim, Brainard went down on the elevator with Lara. And that woman," Trey said. "Jim?" He clicked the button several more times. It didn't work. He tried not to think of the worst that could happen. He tried to think that maybe Brainard and a nurse had gone to get Chilmark for the escort out of Darden. That maybe Lara had gone back to the elevator to go back up for files. That whoever had murdered the secretary had come after Brainard had gone to the canteen. He tried to think of all the things that made the scenario work in Jim's favor.

But he couldn't help thinking of Doc Chilmark. And remembering the photographs of the Flocks, torn apart as if by a lion.

Was the woman with Brainard Bloody Mary?

Trey stared at Hannafin. "Dr. Hannafin, I want you to take the stairs with me. I'd like to ask that you leave those boxes here."

"Trey," she said. "Why is Robert with her? What . . ." Hannafin seemed to be trying to puzzle something out. "What . . . he usually . . . when he left, I thought . . . this morning . . ." Then she pulled herself together. "Okay. Let's get down there."

"Whoever killed Lara is still in the building," Trey said. "The lockdown of the exits ensures it. I want to get you down to the security checkpoint. There will be other guards down there. The building is nearly empty. I can even send someone up here for these boxes for you. I'll just feel better if I get you out of here. But we have to go now. Understood?"

"Oh my God," Dr. Hannafin said. "Robert. She has Robert."

Trey had a strange thought—he had never heard Dr. Brainard called "Robert" by anyone on staff.

4

At the checkpoint at the entrance to Ward D, Jane Laymon had just come in from the outside. As soon as Trey told her about Brainard and Chilmark, Laymon said, "Trey, she's here. You know she's here. It's got to be her. And I think I can guess why she's in the canteen."

CHAPTER THIRTY-FOUR

"His mother's here? Chilmark's mother?" Dr. Hannafin asked. "Holy shit, you're kidding me." Susan Hannafin looked as if she were losing it. Watching the psych techs lose it was one thing—they were expected to go a little nuts given their daily interactions with the worst of the patients. But seeing a psychiatrist of about thirty-six, who had always seemed so together and even on top of everything—watching her start to melt down was unnerving. Trey wasn't sure whether to put his arms around her to keep her feeling safe, or to tell her to snap out of it.

"Doctor," Trey said, "we're going to gather some guards and get down there and get them."

"Down where? Where'd they take him?"

Even as she said this, Trey began to put two and two together.

Dr. Robert Brainard was a career seducer. Hannafin was in love with him. She acted as if she were afraid for her colleague in a way that only lovers felt.

And then he remembered little snippets of thoughts

he'd had when he'd seen them walking out to their cars at the end of a work day. They walked a little too close. Brainard had grinned whenever he saw Susan Hannafin. Even Hannafin and Brainard both working on Doc Chilmark was unusual—the psychiatrists were territorial and didn't often share patients.

He began to feel more sympathy for Hannafin—and Brainard—than he had previously. They had a secret life together, one that they couldn't expose at Darden or one of them would have to leave and find work elsewhere.

It all came to Trey in an instant, and he filed it away in his mind, but it made him see Dr. Hannafin differently than he had just seconds before. The man she loved was in serious danger.

Trey glanced at Jane. "The underground. The lockdown on the ward is in effect. Nobody can get in or out a door. There's one exception. There are three exits from the underground. We don't know if Brainard is aware of them, but if he is, he's likely going to help them get out."

"He doesn't need to know," Jane said. "She knows, Trey. She had maps. She may even have keys. I'm not even sure she wants to escape. I think she wants Brainard. I think she's wanted him for a long time. What's a night cage?"

Trey was about to say something when Hannafin interrupted. "They're cells. Special cells. Outfitted with operating equipment. They were used back in the '40s mainly. Some earlier, some later."

"They're down below, correct?" Laymon asked.

Hannafin nodded. "I took a tour back when I

started here. Darden was famous for them. More lobectomies, thoracic surgeries, and lobotomies were performed here immediately following the second World War than any other hospital in California."

"Do you know where they are?"

Hannafin nodded. "Been there. Second level down. A couple on the first level, but most at the bottom."

"All right, she comes, too," Jane said.

"No, she doesn't," Trey said. "This may end up being a violent takedown. I don't want anybody else's life at risk here."

"I'm going," Hannafin said, shooting a stern look at Trey.

"We have C.O.s here. She'll be fine," Jane said.

Keeping her eyes on Trey, Hannafin said, "Doc Chilmark is under my supervision, and if you believe his mother is also there, I intend to be on hand. Surely the guards—with guns—will prevent any mishap."

"No," Trey said. "No way in hell. Dr. Hannafin, you may have been involved in takedowns, but this is not the same thing at all."

"Two people who are sick are exactly my business," Dr. Hannafin said. "And you still report to me on Chilmark," she added. It felt like a slap in the face to Trey, but he didn't give a damn. All he thought about was Jim, and he hoped the reason that the walkie-talkie didn't work was simply because of a malfunction. He imagined that all Hannafin was thinking about was Dr. Robert Brainard.

When he led them back down the corridor, toward the canteen of Ward D, he had a sick feeling in his stomach.

CHAPTER THIRTY-FIVE

The canteen was empty. The tables were stacked up in a corner as they always were when meals were not being served. Chairs were piled up by the doors to the kitchen.

Jane and three correctional officers went through the kitchen, followed by Trey and Hannafin.

The entry to the underground was open wide.

The light by the stairs was turned on.

Inside the staircase lay Jim Anderson, his legs over the edge of the stairs, his head back on the landing.

His throat was slit so far open that only a thin layer of skin connected it to his body.

CHAPTER THIRTY-SIX

When Trey saw his friend's body, he said to Jane, "I think we need more than three guards to stop these guys." He had to work had to keep his emotions back. They threatened to take him over at any moment. But he was good in an extreme crisis. That was why he had his job. That was why he could do it. He could momentarily put aside those feelings; the adrenaline pumped through him; he could put it in a compartment somewhere in his mind. He'd always been able to do this, at least for the length of time it took to handle what needed to be handled. He was an endurance guy. He could take it in and hold it, and keep it safe until the crisis was past.

But this was different. This felt as if it threatened every atom of his being.

He had loved Jim like no other friend. He had wanted Jim to always be in the world with him.

Always be there. He had taken for granted that Jim would be there. That he and Jim, at Darden, could laugh off any situation that rose to meet them.

They'd worked side by side for more than a decade.

But Trey swallowed the feelings. For now. Later, he would let them take him over and crush him.

Jane turned back toward him, touching him on the shoulder. "I'm sorry, Trey. I'm sorry."

Dr. Hannafin backed up slightly, pressing her hands against her eyes as if willing herself to blot it out.

Trey crouched beside his buddy's body and put his hand on his forehead. He closed his eyes and wished he were thousands of miles away. He wished that Darden State had never held criminal psychopaths.

He wished that he had never passed the walkie-talkie to Jim at all.

Please God, let Jim be in heaven. Let him be someplace better. Please. Please.

After a few seconds, he rose, wiping at his eyes, and said to Jane, "Let's get them. Now."

"Trey, I want you two to stay up here. We'll be fine. We will. But I can't risk your lives next. We may have to do any number of things to stop the two of them. Do you understand?"

Trey nodded.

Jane glanced over at Dr. Hannafin, who had sunk to the floor, her face in her hands. "She needs you up here. This is no longer a takedown situation. We have to assume that they're going to kill Brainard and anyone else they have."

"Who else could they have?" he asked.

Then he saw the large videocamera, set behind the door back into Darden's canteen. "Fuck," he said. "Jim mentioned who else. They have Lance Victor. The reporter. They have at least two people with them. Brainard and Victor."

"Okay," Jane said. "Well, we've got guns. We'll stop them any way we have to. They're delusional. It can be handled, if we're careful. If we take it slow and easy. We'll get the two guys back. They've had it easy so far, Trey. Don't worry. They're using knives right now. We'll get them." Then, to the guards who flanked her on the stairs, she said, "Okay, guys, let's go."

CHAPTER THIRTY-SEVEN

Doc Chilmark held the gun he'd taken from Floyd Nelson's holster against the small of Lance Victor's back. "Keep going."

"Please," Lance whimpered. "Please."

"You making a movie?" Doc asked. "You better be making a movie. Make a movie with your eyes. Everything you see, just put it in the movie."

Lance glanced about the corridor, which was poorly lit. In various rooms, he saw a shadowy darkness. "Where are you taking me?"

"Not you. You're just along for the ride," Mary Chilmark said. "Just shut up. If you shut up, we'll all be fine."

Mary Chilmark had already blindfolded Dr. Brainard using a strip of his jacket. She pushed him along, making him carry her large paper bag in his hands, which they'd bound with wrist restraints she'd brought with her. His left hand, which had been jabbed with the sharp pick she carried, had stopped bleeding.

"Mary, I want you to listen to me before this goes any further," Dr. Brainard said, his voice well-modulated, belying the sweat that poured from him and the slight tremble of his chin.

"Just shut up," she said, pushing him along. "Just keep walking and keep it shut."

CHAPTER THIRTY-EIGHT

Trey stood at the top of the long stairway down into the uppermost level of the underground, watching Jane and the guards go first through the main hall. The lights were fairly bright—a blessing for a hunt like this—and he could see them all the way until they'd passed down the end of the first corridor.

Hannafin, behind him, asked, "There are so many tunnels down there. They could hide anywhere if they wanted to."

"Jane'll get 'em. She's good. I've seen her in action."

"I'm sorry about your friend."

Trey turned around and leaned against the railing. "Thanks."

"It's awful to lose someone you care about," she said, and then covered her mouth slightly, as if catching herself.

"I'm sorry about your friend, too," Trey said.

Hannafin looked at him as if startled. She didn't say anything for a few seconds. Then, "Oh."

"Don't worry," Trey said as warmly as he could. "They'll get them. They'll bring them back up."

The doctor's face looked as if a cloud had passed over it, and she closed her eyes. Trey guessed that she was fighting back tears. "We just couldn't talk about it. Not to anyone here."

"Sure. I understand," Trey said. "I've seen office romances before."

"It's not like that."

"I'm sorry. I didn't mean it the way it sounded." He reached over to her and rested his hand lightly on her shoulder. "It'll be okay, though."

She glanced down over the railing. "Could you do me a favor?"

"Sure."

"When they bring them back up. If Robert's okay. Could we still keep it a secret?"

"Of course," he said.

"I don't talk about my love life," she said. "I guess now's not the time to start."

Trey sat on the first step down and looked out over the hall below, glancing up and down the first of many corridors to see what he could see. Old notes posted decades before still remained behind glass frames. Debris lay in the corners. Desks were piled up, and old gray carpeting lay in rolls of mildew near the entrance to what was probably once an administrator's office.

"It's funny."

"What?" she asked.

"I don't even hear footsteps."

"It's the way sound goes. It's all . . . muffled down there. You've been through the whole thing?"

"Some of it," he said. "Just a bit. I never liked going down there."

"It's not so bad," she said. "It's like an archaeological dig of psychiatry's sedimentary layers. This level is mainly '40s and '50s. It's the second level down that gives me the creeps. It's hard to believe what doctors used to do to people down there. I felt like I had found the ancient city of . . . Troy . . . or something the first time I went down. I felt I could practically see the people who had worked there. And the ones who had lived there."

"I know you're scared," he said. "Me too. But they'll come through this."

"I know they'll be all right," Hannafin said, as if it was a prayer. "I know it."

They remained there, looking down, and after nearly ten minutes, the lights below them went out completely.

CHAPTER THIRTY-NINE

Jane felt nervous as hell as she led the guards down the corridor. She glanced in the rooms—each well lit, and each containing what seemed to her to be fully stocked medical supplies. Now and then she glanced over her shoulder slightly to make sure the officers were with her. She didn't know them, and she sure as hell wasn't sure how good they were with their guns or tazers. She just hoped it would go easy and they'd get a good jump on Bloody Mary and Doc.

Thick wires hung down from the pipes overhead, and there were stepladders and ceiling debris in some of the larger rooms. She assumed it was from recent work being done. When she glanced up at the ceiling of one of the rooms, which looked like an operating theater, she thought she saw a running grate up top. Then, to the left, she saw a long room with several metal beds all stacked up against each other. If it hadn't been for the peeling paint on the wall and the bits of plaster that had dropped over time, she would've thought this was a fully functioning ward.

It was like a storage closet time machine.

She looked back—the guys with her looked scared shitless. For C.O.s working with the criminally insane, they didn't exhibit any sense that this was going to be a routine takedown.

Her depth perception was off, too. It was the problem of her eye. A psychopath already had taken one eye, and she didn't intend to have another one drawn out by a whole new set of psychos.

When they got to the end of the corridor, where it shifted to the left, she pressed her back against the wall. She gave her guys a quick glance that said "be ready for anything"—and then, holding up her Glock, she swiftly turned the corner.

She swore under her breath.

Another long hallway loomed, and it looked as if at the end of it, it branched off in two directions.

The lights here were old hanging bulbs with metal back-shades above them. *Must've been fancy in the '50s,* she thought.

A series of rooms lined the new corridors, and each doorway was empty of even a door. As Jane went along, she had to check each room in case the Chilmarks were hiding in them.

She turned back to the other officers, waving for them to keep up.

When she looked in one of the rooms, she saw at least a dozen large traps—and each had one dead rat in them. Another room was filled with wheelchairs. Still another had broken glass all over the floor.

She moved faster—she could see their footsteps in the dust on the floor.

Just as she got to the end, she saw a man kneeling down to the left of the wall's edge. She drew up her gun. He had blond hair, tamped down with sweat and what she assumed was blood. His face dripped with blood, and his hands were behind his back. A strip of cloth had been wrapped tightly around his mouth, and there was blood coming from his lips. He was breathing through his nose such that his nostrils flared and then closed as if he were gasping for breath. His eyes widened as he stared at her.

A *hostage*, she thought, and immediately pulled back against the wall and turned about to tell the guards behind her.

The lights flickered—just once.

She saw a blur of movement as a woman leapt from one of the doorways they'd passed, some large metal instrument in her hands, coming for the guard who was farthest back.

The lights overhead began flickering again—this time almost like the strobe lights upstairs. She noticed it all at once—the hostage, then the woman leaping as if she were a lion going after its prey; the two guards directly behind her saw her expression and began to turn to look back.

And then they were plunged into darkness.

CHAPTER FORTY

"Someone's shut off the switch," Trey said.

"The guards wouldn't do it," Hannafin said. "They wouldn't."

Trey strained to listen, as if he'd hear their voices.

"I hate waiting here," she said. "Just waiting. God knows what's happening."

"It's just the lights. Maybe Jane shut them off for a reason."

"I know where it is," Hannafin said. "The switch. It's in that wheelchair graveyard area."

"The what?"

"The main switch. There's a bunch of old wheelchairs just collecting dust. If you wait, if it works right, the emergency lights will come on in a few minutes."

The only light that entered the stairwell was from the door behind them.

"It's strange in the dark," she said. "My main studies have been about seeing what we do exposed to daylight. The secrets. The dark places. But if you sit in the dark sometimes, you remember things. Things you might want to forget sometimes."

"It'll be okay," he said, sensing the weight of her words—she was thinking too deeply, too seriously. He wanted to try to offer her some comfort.

"Other doctors here knew we'd been a couple," she said. "But we've been doing our best to hide it."

"Sure. I never guessed. Well, I mean, 'til now."

"Everybody keeps secrets from somebody."

As she spoke, he felt the darkness below them—and the unanswered questions it posed—was not worth dwelling on. He sat there, wishing he could lighten her mood. Wishing whatever darkness she now felt within her mind could be allowed to escape into the light of day. He remembered what Brainard had told him about psychiatrists. How they sometimes were in the profession because they themselves needed to untangle their minds.

"Trey," Hannafin said. "I'm worried about him. All of them down there. Even Doc Chilmark."

"They have flashlights," Trey said. "Just like this one. Don't worry." He drew a long slender flashlight up and flicked it on. He shined it down into the dark. The light bounced off peeling walls and the open cabinets and storage closets.

"The emergency lights should be up by now."

"Jane knows what she's doing," Trey said.

A sound like a distant pop. Then another.

And another.

Gunfire.

CHAPTER FORTY-ONE

Jane felt heat rise beneath her skin as she turned around. She couldn't shoot. She couldn't even see. There was the sound of a scuffle behind her; one of the men shouted. There was another shot and a brief brightness. For the barest moment, she thought she felt a hand on her neck. She wrenched away from it, pivoting around to bring her gun to eye level, ready to shoot. Her hands trembled. *You've been through worse. Hang on. Hang on. You can do it. You can get through it.*

Silence.

She crouched down, figuring she was less of a target closer to the floor. Then she lay on her stomach, keeping her elbows bent and holding the gun upward in case she detected movement near her.

A terrible sound began somewhere not far from her in the dark.

It was a slicing and ripping, and then the wet slurp of a body being cut open.

She heard a groan, but it was faint as if it were far away.

CHAPTER FORTY-TWO

Susan Hannafin said, "We've got to get down there, Trey. If they've shot anybody . . . the patients, or . . . well, if anyone's hurt, I've got to."

"Dr. Hannafin, no," Trey said.

But Hannafin stepped around him and began running down the stairs. He kept the flashlight on her as she went. He didn't know what had come over her, and part of him wanted to race back down to the checkpoint at Ward D, but he didn't like the odds of any of this.

"Damn it," Trey said.

He thought of Jim Anderson, just beyond the doorway behind him. He thought of what he would've done to save him, if he'd only gone to the canteen with him.

What two people could do that one could not.

He thought of Jane, and even of Dr. Brainard and Lance Victor. Their faces in his mind. He imagined them dead, throats slit like Jim's had been. Nothing

251

but meat in the end. Nothing but a plaything for the human monsters who couldn't even understand what they were doing when they killed.

He thought of the good and bad of life, and wanted the good to come out on top this time.

He followed Hannafin into the underground, calling out to her to wait for him. "I've got the flashlight, damn it, hang on," he said.

CHAPTER FORTY-THREE

Lights flickered up from the edges of the hallways. They bathed the peeling walls in a hazy blue. For Jane, it flattened out her vision further—she could no longer tell the distance of objects and people. She scooched behind a doorway, rising to a crouching position, keeping her Glock at the ready.

Down the hallway, the patches of blue light did not permeate every square foot of the hall—the emergency lights were only at the ends of the corridor and in every other room along it.

Behind her, she saw two bodies on the floor. One of the guards lay on his back and continued to shiver as blood poured from his throat; his gut also had been ripped open. Another, several feet behind him, was so covered with blood she couldn't even see his face or scalp.

She felt a panic seize her as she glanced back and forth, trying to make out who else was there.

Then, from down at the nearest end of the hall, one of the guards stepped forward. He looked at his feet as he came. She had not gotten a good look at him when he'd joined up with her to explore this area. He was young—too young to be facing what he now had to face.

Behind him, the woman.

Bloody Mary.

Focus. Come on, focus, Jane kept telling herself. But there was something about the blue lights and the shadows between them that wasn't helping with her vision.

Bloody Mary must have something in his back. A gun. Something, Jane thought. *Okay, you'll get through this. You will. If you aim, you'll miss him. You'll wing her. But that may be enough for her to drop him, and then you'll get a clear shot.*

"We're going to perform surgery today," Mary said, her voice calm and smooth as if none of this had any effect on her. "Today. My son, he's a doctor. He's a healer. There are too many to be healed in this world."

"Let him go," Jane whispered, then repeated herself in a normal tone. Or as normal as she could get it. She held her gun steady. She began to look for ways of distracting Bloody Mary so that she'd let the guard go for a split second.

She heard a noise behind her. Quickly, she turned her head to the side.

The hostage she'd seen in the hall on his knees was far back in the shadows of the room she'd chosen. She could just make him out. Her eye began tearing up. Or else the sweat on her forehead had dripped down into it. She swiped at it with her hand.

The man with the gag over his mouth had begun

crawling toward her. She had no time to signal him to stay where he was. She had to turn around and keep watching Bloody Mary.

When she glanced out into the hall, Bloody Mary had stepped closer with the guard in front of her as a shield.

Suddenly, the young guard began trembling, and his eyes went wide. His legs seemed to be buckling; Jane saw his body collapse as if he had just lost all muscle coordination.

The guard's mouth opened wide in a scream, but no sound came out.

He dropped to the ground.

Bloody Mary stood there, her dress soaked with blood, her hair wild, and a long cutting saw of some kind that had scissorlike attachments.

Jane knew she had a split second to act. She took fast aim, but heard someone running toward her from behind.

She had to turn—she had no choice. As she did, she saw that she and the hostage had not been the only ones in the room.

Doc came running for her and at the very last second she saw the tazer. Before she could react fast enough, her gun went off in her hand, and she felt the bite of electric shock when the probes of the tazer connected with her left hip.

CHAPTER FORTY-FOUR

Doc got down on all fours beside the woman who'd just dropped. "A cop," he said. "Cool."

Behind him, Lance Victor began to make bleating noises under his gag. Doc turned around. He pointed his finger at him. "You just keep still from now on. You hear?"

As he looked at Lance, Doc was sure he saw a shadow behind him. Not like the other shadows when people got healed. These were shadows that lived down here.

The ghosts the other patient had told him about.

From the doorway, his mother reached down and stroked his scalp. He felt good when she touched him. Safe. He looked up at her. "I see shadows all around us."

"Good ones?" she asked.

"I think so. I don't feel the fears. Not like I did in the dark. I felt them when the lights went out. I felt them crawling from all the cracks in the walls."

"I'm sorry about the dark," she said. "But we had to shut it down. They might've hurt you."

"I know," he said. "You kept me safe. Where'd you put my father?"

"Back there," Mary said, cocking her head to the side to indicate any number of rooms behind her. Beyond the bodies of the guards. "Come on, sweetheart. Let's go."

"I have your bag," Doc said, pointing toward a stack of magazines in a corner. Just visible over the tops of them was the grocery bag.

"Good. Get it. I'll go get your father. We'll heal him soon."

"What about this one?" Doc swiveled around to look at Lance Victor, who had slipped to the floor and could not get back up with his hands tied behind him.

"Yes," she said.

"And this one?" He looked down at Jane, who lay there, her eyes closed.

"She'll be up soon. Let's get her bound. Check the supply closet up the hall. I bet there's some restraints still in it," his mother said.

CHAPTER FORTY-FIVE

Trey switched the flashlight off when the blue emergency lights came up. Dr. Hannafin walked ahead of him.

"Slow down," he said.

"They're down there. You heard the shots. That they haven't come back . . ." She stopped and glanced back at him.

"Dr. Hannafin," he said. "Susan. Let's go back up. The lights are up. Jane and the other guards know what they're doing. I'll take you back upstairs. We'll see if the ward doors are open yet. There'll be someone to help them if anything happened."

"I know where they're taking him," Dr. Hannafin said. She no longer seemed like a superior, a psychiatrist. For the first time, in that pale blue light of the corridor, he saw her as a frightened person. A woman who had held something back. "He told me about her. He told me about what she does. What they did. He never lied to me, Trey. He loved her. Too many years ago to bother me. He loved her. A patient. He brought her here, and they . . . they did things. Nothing sick. Not like what was in her head, I'm sure. She fucked with him then. She's fucking with him now. She's going to gut him, Trey. She told him that years ago. She told him after she'd been released. After he worked hard to get her released. Believing she had been badly treated. Believing her lies that the patients she'd killed had provoked her attack and had keyed into the triggers of her psychosis. He believed she was a victim, Trey. Oh God." Susan slid down to the floor, her face in her hands.

Trey went and sat beside her, putting his arm around her. "It's all right. It'll be all right."

Susan began weeping. "Please forgive me, I can't believe I'm doing this," she said. She pushed her tears away with her fingers. "I'm not weak. I'm not. I hate doing this. But ever since they brought him in, I knew."

"That Doc is his son."

Susan nodded. "I knew it was all there. I knew she was out there again. I thought we were both safe."

Trey felt a chill spread over him. "You felt unsafe before?"

Susan Hannifin didn't reply.

"Dr. Hannafin," he said.

"She came to his house once," Hannafin said, and then cleared her throat. "She came to his house. I was there, but he wasn't. I didn't know who she was. I was just staying for the weekend. She said she was an old girlfriend. Robert has had many girlfriends. Lovers. I'm not blind to that. I've been around the block, too. You know, you can have a medical degree, be top of your class, and research the human mind into its darkest corner. And still, still . . . you just don't fathom what you yourself are willing to go through when you love someone. You reach a point when you say to yourself, 'I forgive him.' I can move beyond this. His past is nothing. He was younger then and foolish. It's none of my business. But she told me about their games."

Trey drew her close to him. "Susan, let's go back up. We don't need to be here."

"They played games, she told me. Games where he'd tie her up. Games where he and another doctor—the one she married, Massey—tied her up on a table here. They took turns. Well . . ." She wiped at her face again. "Well, I knew it was a lie. It was a lie. I know Robert well enough. We've been seeing each other for almost six years. I know his . . . his ins and outs. He's not like that. But the worst thing that she told me was that he had asked me to play games with him, too. She knew it. She said we were alike. We both loved him. We both would do anything for him." She paused, then heaved a sigh. "I knew that much was true."

Trey leaned back against the wall. He didn't want to hear any more. None of it surprised him, and he passed no judgment on anyone else's private lives. He didn't like hearing about them. He didn't like hearing this story, either. He wished she had never begun talking about it.

He felt an overwhelming sadness for her as they sat there. She loved Robert Brainard too much. And Brainard was basically a jerk and possibly a creep. Maybe he was the smartest man alive. Maybe he made love like Don Juan. But he wasn't worth what this woman had put into him. She loved him above all else. Trey could tell by the way she said his name. Some women did that. They loved their men beyond their own sense of happiness.

Trey felt he loved Carly like that, too. He understood. He would put her first every single time he could. He'd failed her sometimes, but as he thought of his wife in that twisted corridor, he sent a little prayer to her and to the kids. *Dad'll be safe. Dad loves you. Honey, I love you. I'll be home again. I promise.*

"I never mentioned to him that she came by. I never mentioned what she said to me. Until Chilmark came in, I didn't really have to think about it. She was elsewhere. Even when Dr. Massey died, well, Robert had cut himself off from that lunatic years before I met him. But when I saw her picture in the files yesterday, Trey. When I saw that face again, I remembered her well from her visit to his house. I remember how she told me that we had a lot in common. And when I asked her what she meant, she didn't have to tell me. It wasn't just him. It was that other thing. That thing women don't talk about with men. Or in their jobs. It was that thing where despite all our training, all our education, and disposing of the nonsense of thinking the man is everything and the woman is nothing . . . sometimes, certain women give it all for a man. Sometimes, the things a man shares with a woman in the dark becomes a surrender of what is right and wrong."

Then she fell silent, and Trey was glad she did. He didn't want to hear about her inner life. He preferred to think of her as a ward psychiatrist, not as a woman.

Not as Susan, but as Dr. Hannafin, who kept her distance most of the time. Professional. Above reproach. Perhaps nobody was that professional or that untouchable in life.

She had acquired a soul here with Trey. Beneath the hospital. She had opened up under the stress of the moment. She had shown him a little of the private woman he would never have otherwise known.

He almost grinned, thinking of what Jim Anderson would've said. *"Hannafin's a friggin' lunatic. Can't always tell the doctors from the patients in here."* That's what he would've said. Trey held back a breath, trying not to let the grief of Jim's murder overwhelm him. *Christ, this is a sorry place to be. Under a building. A fire might be sweeping over us soon. Within here, two very psychopathic killers with delusions of medical expertise and an entire world for their madness.*

Trey felt as if the two of them were alone in an underworld, a city of the dead—of psychiatry's past folly and vanity and monstrosity. He remembered Fallon with his talk of ghosts down here, and it would not have surprised him if they did, indeed, wander these halls. The tubercular who had died here, the mentally retarded who had once been hidden away and forgotten, the mentally ill who had the unfortunate circumstance to be alive before the prescription drug revolution, and others who society deemed outcasts needing hospitalization deep in the ground just to hide them from the rest of the community.

Finally, Trey said softly, "Everyone has secret places. I understand. Let's go back. All right? We'll get help."

She wiped her eyes again, and took his hand as he rose.

From somewhere ahead of them, the bloodcurdling scream of a man echoed along the walls.

CHAPTER FORTY-SIX

1

"You do anything—run, hide, anything," Mary said, her arm raised up, her fist around a long slender ice pick pointed to Lance Victor's head, "I will be on you. I will trepan your brain and draw it out for you to look at while you're dying. Do you understand?"

Lance Victor nodded vigorously.

Mary lowered the pick, and with her free hand reached up and adjusted Lance's gag, which had slipped down from the lips she had only recently sliced with her scalpel. From one of the supply closets, Doc had brought out an array of old moth-worn strait-jackets and ankle hobbles that were heavier than the modern ones he had been used to wearing in his home cage.

He secured the jacket on Lance, then hobbled his ankles together. Then he went to restrain the police-woman, who had begun showing signs of reviving from the second tazer shot he'd given her.

"Your father took me to the night cages," Mary said. "When I was young. They're downstairs. It may be dark. Do you understand?"

Doc nodded.

"We'll heal him. All of them," she said.

"I know. I can feel a healing coming to me," he said.

"I will never leave you in the dark," his mother said.

Stepping over one of the dead guards, she went back to the room full of wheelchairs to get the man she had loved her whole life, the father of her child, in the room where she'd secured him.

2

Once Doc had Jane Laymon all wrapped up tight, with restraints and a gag, she opened her good eye, watching him. He still had the tazer, and pressed it point-blank into the same hip where he'd shot her before. He squeezed the trigger, and the prongs went into her.

Her eye fluttered for a moment or two, and her body convulsed.

He glanced back at the room. There were little metal cabinetlike doors on the wall.

As he dragged her toward them, he was nearly positive that she watched him.

"It's okay," Doc said to her. "It's okay. We'll come back for you. We will. I'll heal you, too. Don't worry. We just have too much to take with us here."

He opened one of the cabinets and drew out a long tray. Inside, it looked almost like a metal oven. He stretched his arm all the way in.

It was the perfect size.

3

Once he'd put Laymon on the flat surface, he pushed it in and shut the drawer.

"It's a morgue," he said aloud. "It's perfect." He grabbed an open lock from the pile on the floor and although it was rusted, it still closed. He put it through the loop of metal at the morgue cabinet door. "Don't be afraid," he said to the door. "You're safe there."

CHAPTER FORTY-SEVEN

1

Trey ran with Susan Hannafin down the hallway, toward the scream they'd heard. As they reached the end of one corridor, they turned into another.

Hannafin shrieked when she saw the bodies on the ground.

Trey came up behind her.

2

Three of the guards were accounted for, but there was no sign of Jane. Trey held out a hope.

He grabbed a gun from beside each of the bodies. "You ever use these?"

"Never," she said.

"First time for everything," he said. "Let's go. Let's go. We may not have any time now."

He ran ahead, quickly ducking in and out of rooms, hoping to see a sign, something that might indicate

Jane was alive. That she had survived. He saw rooms full of chairs, and one that had strips of newspaper clippings all over the floor; still another seemed to be the morgue of the underground—a wall that was made out of cheap metal with rust along its drawers. Another room had all kinds of bottles, large and small, set in rows throughout it as if they'd been collected from all over the hospital and stored here.

Finally, following the trail of blood they reached what seemed to be the dead end of the ward.

"There's a door off there." Susan pointed toward one of the utility rooms. "To the next level down."

"They're taking them to the night cages," Trey said.

3

Looking through the doorway into the lower section, Trey saw that it was completely dark. He switched on his flashlight and kept the gun in his right hand as he stepped down onto the metal stairs.

Susan followed him. They went carefully down into the dark hole of a room below.

About three steps from the bottom, Trey missed a step, stumbling. His flashlight flew out of his hand.

He fell down to the bottom step, hitting his head hard against the floor below. His gun rolled across the floor.

4

"You okay?" Hannafin asked. She felt her way down the last few steps, and got down on all fours, reaching for the flashlight. When she had it, she pointed it along the floor until she found Trey. "Trey?"

"It's okay," he said. "Get the gun. It's . . . it's over there." He pointed somewhere off to the right.

After she'd helped him up, and he had the gun again and the flashlight, she said, "There are six tunnels down here. Not all of them are functioning."

"What's that mean?" he asked.

"Some go out under the grounds, beyond the buildings. Some have caved in over the years, so they're nothing but rubble at one end."

"We can't get lost down here, can we?" he asked.

5

There were rows of metal beds along the corridor in the second level down. Trey shined his flashlight along the wall.

"The night cages," she said. "There are nine of them. Three here. Six at the end of the hallway that goes to the tunnels."

"It's like a catacombs," he said, directing the flashlight's beam along the various avenues that shot off from the main hallway. The other pathways were narrow and must have made the patients who had been virtually imprisoned down there feel as if they were buried alive at times.

There were three closed doors in a row along one side of the wall. Along the other, the therapy rooms that had been used for hydrotherapy and minor operations.

"Lobectomies. Thoracic surgery. Lobotomies." Trey pointed the flashlight farther down to the long corridor. What looked almost like dried human feces was smeared along the crack-filled walls. At the end of the hallway was the entrance to where the pipes and the tunnels intersected. "The major one—shock treatment—was upstairs. It's hard to think of all this as minor surgery."

"What was that?" she asked.

"What?"

"Over there. By the door."

"Which door?" he whispered, feeling a chill within him. *Think of Jane. Think of Brainard. Hell, think of Lance Victor. Don't be afraid. Don't let the darkness win.*

She took the flashlight from him and shined it to the second night cage door. It was open slightly, and it might've even been moving. It was as if a light wind pushed at the door from the inside, a draft that kept it opening and closing, almost imperceptibly.

Trey stepped forward, but kept the gun held up, ready to point it toward anybody. He crossed the large room, keeping the light on the door.

When he got to the night cage, he reached for the door handle. It was slick and wet. He drew it outward, shining the light inside.

The night cage was small, with a low ceiling that had a grate in it. Above the grate was a metal fan for ventilation. In one corner was a hole that had once been the toilet. In another corner a shelf that must've served for a bed, although there was no mattress or blanket on it.

Written on the wall in a dark smear: *Tumors Malignant.*

Trey took one step into the room.

And that's when he felt something grasp at his ankles.

He looked down. A shadow there. He shone the light on it.

He didn't identify the man right away. And then he knew. It was Lance Victor, the television reporter. But it took a long time for Trey to realize this, because there was so much blood along the man's back, which had been split open to expose his spinal cord.

They had ripped his skin from his back and dug into him.

Chapter Forty-eight

Because Lance's fingers still moved, Trey knelt down beside him, setting the flashlight on the floor to cast light across the dying man's body.

"It's Lance, come on," he called to Hannafin, but in the few seconds it took for her to get there, the man had died.

Hannafin crouched beside Trey and put her hand on his back. "Let's go," she said. "Trey, we have to go find them."

"I know," he said. But he could not leave the dead man yet. He felt an ache within him. And an anger that had grown since finding Jim dead upstairs. A fury. *Please be alive, Jane. Please. I will find you. I promise. I will stop this. Somehow.*

"I wonder about the fire," Hannafin said suddenly. "I wonder if it's reached the grounds above us."

"Maybe we're safer down here," Trey said. Then he felt the slight madness in having said that. He began to feel a little light-headed. Something within him was changing down in this place. Some sense of human decency had begun to vanish. He wanted to tell Hannafin about it, but he was sure she wouldn't understand. He wanted to tell her what he felt rising in his craw—in that primitive place inside him.

He had faced psychopaths before.

He sometimes even pretended to understand their delusions.

But not this time. These were worse than predatory animals.

Bloody Mary was like an alien species. If she could do this, if she could twist her son's soul into doing this, doing it quickly, doing it without remorse, without a sense of empathy for the suffering of the ones beneath her knives and saws . . . she wasn't even human anymore.

Not in his eyes.

Years of training exploded for him.

"Let's check every night cage," he said.

Hannafin began making a strange sound.

He stood up, grasping her elbow. "Susan?"

"I want them dead," she said.

"I know. Me too."

"I want to kill them," Hannafin said, her voice nearly a growl. "I'm not supposed to think that. But it's what I want to do."

"Yeah, I know," he said. "Let's go."

CHAPTER FORTY-NINE

1

Doc had warned his mother that others would follow, but she told him that it all would be taken care of. "We're healers," she said. "What we bring to them is good. They understand."

Doc had spent the better part of the past half hour gathering more of the surgical tools they'd need. The place was full of all kinds of little hammers and picks and long saws that cut just like scissors, which he was fairly sure had been used as bonesaws. He'd spent most of his childhood and all his adolescence studying medical practices. He had a good feel for the tools of the trade, large and small. But as he went down one particular tunnel, he thought he saw someone standing nearby. He didn't exactly see the person at first. He felt it the way he always felt the shadows. In the area where they had decided to perform the major surgery, the red lights were on, and these comforted him. But he could not see the shadow even in the glow of the light.

"Who's there?" he asked.

He tried to ignore the feeling that he was being watched. He didn't think it was one of the night fears. His mother had told him they couldn't find him this far down. But when he opened the door of what had once been an office, he was sure it was a little girl. Hadn't the patient above talked about seeing her? A little girl who was dead. A little girl who had not passed over into the light.

He opened the cabinets, looking for just the right tools for the surgery. At one point he caught a glimpse of her in a broken mirror that hung on the back of one of the cabinet doors.

She had a yellow-blue aura about her. He just saw a little bit of her face. He turned around quickly.

She didn't try to hide.

In the light that she gave off he saw the shadows of others who had lived here and had died here without moving toward the light of heaven.

"Hello," Doc Chilmark said to her.

2

"There's a little girl down the tunnel a ways," he told his mother when he'd brought the rolled up towel full of instruments back to the night cage where they had tied his father down to the table. "She's dead. But she's like a bright shadow."

CHAPTER FIFTY

Dr. Brainard looked up at Mary Chilmark's face, bathed in red light. The gag was still tight over his mouth, and he felt pain all over his arms and legs. He was sure a rib had been broken as they'd pushed him and thrown him around on his journey down to this room.

He tried to rein in his fear. He resolved to remain calm. He felt a sense of peace. If he could just get the gag off. If he could speak to her.

She operated off delusion and pleasure. She did not desire pain for herself. He knew that.

If he could just speak to her. Reassure her. Talk to her about what had happened.

He knew that, given her personality type, she would respond.

But the gag stayed on, and so nothing was said.

When Doc returned, Mary began to open Brainard's already torn shirt. "I'll prep the patient, Doc."

CHAPTER FIFTY-ONE

"Here's how it goes," Bloody Mary said as she tore the shirt back, and then undid his pants, slipping them down as far as she could before the restraints that held Brainard to the operating table got in the way. "Robert, your son has grown into an excellent healer. A real doctor. Not one made by some school. But a natural-born one."

She leaned over Brainard's body and rested her hand on Doc's face. Doc felt warmth flood him. She hadn't touched him like that since the last time he'd laid in her arms. She was purity. Purity and love in the flesh.

On the table, Brainard tried to mumble through the gag.

"The way I see it," Doc said, grinning to his nurse, "there's a lot of work to be done here."

"Yes. Let's get started," she said. "Do you remember how this goes, Doc?"

Doc nodded. "Like the Flock woman. With the malignancy."

"That's right," his mother said. Then she went to get what she'd brought all this way in her grocery bag.

Doc heard a voice behind him and turned, afraid that someone would stop his healing.

It was the dead girl he had seen before. She smiled at him, and he nodded back. There were others with her as well, although he couldn't see them as clearly. He said to his mother, "They're with us."

"Who?" Mary asked.

"The ones who never left here. When he gets healed," he said, nodding toward his father, "will he stay here?"

"I don't know," his mother said. She brought something from the bag—it was wrapped in newspaper. "He might go to the light."

"I'm not scared down here," Doc said.

"You shouldn't be," Bloody Mary said. "It's where I brought you into me."

CHAPTER FIFTY-TWO

1

Trey heard the noise first. It wasn't quite a shout, and it wasn't a scream. But it was as if someone had called out in the red-lit pathways between the night cages. He followed it, running ahead of Hannafin. When he reached a door that was slightly ajar, he let his adrenaline take over, and held up the gun, figuring he'd have to aim for Bloody Mary first, since Doc could be subdued. He thought about this within seconds, and then pushed the door open.

The operating table was in the center of the room.

The restraints at the uppermost and lowermost parts of the table had been torn open. Blood-stained towels were stacked as if underneath a patient's body.

But there was no one.

Whomever had been operated on was no longer in the room. When Hannafin caught up to him, he had her turn the flashlight into the dark corners of the room. They both heard a slight noise that sounded like a child blowing milk bubbles.

There, beneath the operating table and back against the wall, was Dr. Brainard.

Naked.

Clutching what seemed to be his belly, which had been greatly distended.

Trey quickly moved to him, getting down on his knees. "Doctor. Dr. Brainard?"

In the flashlight's glare Dr. Brainard looked as if he were eighty years old rather than in his late fifties. Bubbles of blood came from between his lips, and the whites of his eyes showed as he blinked in the light.

Trey tried to keep the feeling of nausea within him.

He could not help looking at the man's purplish, blood-smeared, distended belly.

It had a row of sutures or stitches—but made with material that seemed like twine—holding his stomach together.

They had cut into his stomach.

"Dear God," Trey said. "Dear God."

2

He stayed with Dr. Brainard until the man died in Susan Hannafin's arms.

They had put something inside Brainard's stomach. They had opened him up and put something inside him that had caused swelling and then they'd brutally sewn him up again.

Trey hoped it wasn't the dead fetus that had been killed two days before at the Flocks'.

But she's insane. She belonged in Darden State all along. She didn't belong out in the world. She didn't belong where other people lived. She belonged on meds, in a hospital for the criminally insane.

Trey hoped he was wrong. But it didn't matter to Brainard. The psychiatrist was dead now.

From behind him, he heard Susan Hannafin's voice cry out in alarm. As he spun about quickly, he felt something sharp go into his ribs, and for just a moment he saw Bloody Mary's face above him, the red glow of light all around her.

The face of madness.

Then he passed out, hearing Susan Hannafin screaming in a way he'd never heard another human being scream in his life.

CHAPTER FIFTY-THREE

1

Doc had to slam Hannafin's head into the wall three times before she was knocked out. "This the bitch?" he asked his mother, who was across the room with Trey Campbell.

His mother nodded.

"I should heal her now," Doc said. "Right now."

"Get her safe," Bloody Mary said to her son. "Baby, get her safe. We have lots of time. It's a big day at the hospital. One operation after another."

2

Susan Hannafin awoke sitting up on the operating table in one of the night cages. She was alone. Her head ached like hell. She had been put in leg restraints, and her arms were strapped behind her, attached to a small lead that was hooked to the wall.

She looked up to a cagelike ceiling, and beyond it, the red emergency light.

She felt as if a truck had hit her. She called out for Trey, but there was no answer.

She spent the better part of an hour struggling to get free of the restraints.

3

Jane Laymon regained consciousness. She felt as though she were buried alive, but soon came to terms with the space she'd been put into. Some narrow morgue-like drawer, perhaps. She wasn't sure. She tried to move, but realized that the numbness in her arms had something to do with the straitjacket they'd put her in. Her ankles, too, were tied together.

She felt weak; her mouth was dry; her throat was sore; and her left hip was still a little tender from the tazer burn.

The space she was in felt warm—probably the air. Probably not enough fresh air coming in.

Her heels pressed against wall. If she pushed herself up slightly, her head was pressed against wall also.

They put me in here somehow.

She remembered her last sight was of what looked like a series of drawers along a wall. A small morgue of some kind.

"All right. You didn't kill me. That's good for me. Bad for you," she whispered.

She began bending her knees. She could bend them halfway to her stomach. She stretched them back down to touch what she hoped was the drawer opening. Not a wall, but something that could move out-ward.

If she could move it.

She bent her knees as far as they'd go toward her stomach, then kicked them down to the other side.

Her shoes slammed against the base of the drawer.

It gave slightly.

Okay, she thought. *A thousand more of these, and maybe I get out of here.*

CHAPTER FIFTY-FOUR

1

Trey awoke on a table. They had brought him into his own night cage.

He saw the red light above the cage.

He looked first to the left, then the right. He felt a soreness along his jaw. They'd tied a gag over his mouth.

Restraints at his wrists. His ankles.

His lower right side hurt.

She stabbed me. Great.

He heard footsteps coming into the room. He strained his neck, looking up from the table, and had to lay his head back down.

He looked to the left—there was a small kidney-shaped tray.

On it were several instruments. He recognized the little hammer and the pick, as well as the Hay saw—a special saw for cutting the skull and brain pan open.

He knew enough about Bloody Mary's M.O. to realize what he was up for. *Lobotomy or just simple brain surgery. Christ.*

He wondered how much time he had. He knew he had to work his way out of this. He doubted there was anyone left to come to the rescue.

Please, God. Please. Help me. He thought of Carly again—her face. The news of bringing a baby into the world. The shock of it. The surprise. The last look she'd given him the night before. That look of love that he hoped he'd given back to her.

Use what you know, he thought. He remembered enough about at least one escape from restraints to know that there was always a way to do it if you really wanted to. Doc had talked about Houdini and how he had read up on how to get out of restraints. There was a way.

Give me five minutes, he thought. *God, just five minutes. I don't expect you to come out of the wall with a full-blown miracle. Just five minutes and I can do it myself.*

2

As it turned out, he got less than a minute and a half before Bloody Mary came in and leaned over him. Her breath was foul, but at least she'd cleaned the blood from her face. Her dark hair had turned stringy and hung down in his face. "You're vexed," she said. "I can tell." Then she drew back and turned to someone at the door. "Doc? Are you ready for this one? It may be an emergency."

3

"Hello again," Doc Chilmark said. He had a boyish grin on his face as he peered down at Trey. "You should've stayed upstairs. You know that."

Trey nodded. He tried to keep the movement around his hands minimized. He was hoping to draw his hands through the wrist restraints, but it didn't seem to be working. As Doc spoke to him, Trey focused on the edge of the table. He was able to get his hands flopped over it just a bit, on the side with the surgery tray. He felt along the underside of the table, and when he found the metal edge, he rubbed the strap of the restraint against it. *Nice. Keep talking, Doc. Just keep talking.*

Trey ignored the bad stuff he heard: the words said to him about the operation to come, about how the brain could be modified with just the boring of a hole or two. He tried to ignore everything but that one little restraint strap at his wrist, and the slow but steady sawing movement he had going. *Old restraints,* Trey thought. *They're bound to give it up. Bound to tear a little here and there. How many years ago were they used? Forty? Thirty? So long ago and in between time, a lot of possibilities for falling apart.*

He felt that surge of madness again. He looked up at Doc and Bloody Mary. *I can be as crazy as you if I want to be. You had no problem slicing my best friend's throat. No problem with poor Lance. Or Brainard. In fact, you haven't seen crazy until you can see what I can do. I'm gonna go temporary insanity on both your asses.*

Bloody Mary had a long pick in her left hand and a small rounded hammer in her right.

Great. I get a lobotomy. No thanks. No thanks.

He felt the fabric of the restraint that held his right hand give. The sharp metal edge of the table had cut through it.

Trey drew his right arm out from behind him, the restraint flopping to the side, and grabbed Mary Chilmark's hand in midair as she brought the pick toward his eye. He tugged hard with his left hand, and it hurt like hell, but he tore the restraint out completely as he swung around. He felt her strength, which seemed greater than a woman her size should have. He pushed at her arm to get the instrument away from his face. At the same time, Doc Chilmark tried to pull him back down onto the table. Doc punched him hard in the jaw, and Trey fell backward, sliding halfway off the table, his ankle restraints keeping him from rolling completely off it.

Doc reached over to the surgery tray and drew up the trepan and the small hammer that would be used to break a hole in his skull. Trey mustered all his strength and kicked out, tearing at the ankle restraints—and hitting Mary in the gut as she came back at him. But Doc had descended upon him, wrapping his arm around Trey's neck. With his free hand, Doc pressed the Hay saw against Trey's scalp.

Trey felt the slightest feather of pain there and knew that Doc had begun to cut. Blood poured down over Trey's eyes, but he fought back as best he could, knocking Doc backward. Trey managed to drop from the table to the floor, feeling a sickening pain in his head from the cutting Doc had done. He could barely see for the blood that covered his eyes. *You'll get through this. You have to. You have to stop them. You have to. Nobody brought you here. You came here. You weren't meant to die today. Not today, you son-of-a-bitch. You got a kid on the way.*

He rose up again, using every ounce of strength he had. He grabbed the pick from the table and made a half-turn toward Doc.

Mary came up behind Trey, leaping onto his back, knocking him to the floor again, on all fours. She had her weight on him, and she began screaming as if she were a wildcat, her arms around his throat, obscenities flying from her mouth.

Trey crouched back on his knees, took the pick with both hands, and swung it as hard as he could above and behind his head.

He felt it go into the back of Mary's neck.

He didn't stop. He stabbed her again and again and again, his own voice hoarse from shouting through the gag, "Get off me, you bitch! Get off me! Get the fuck off me!"

Finally, her hands loosened at his throat, and he shrugged her off. She landed beside him, on the floor of the night cage.

He rolled over onto his back, too weak to stand, gasping for breath.

He held the pick up to defend himself if Doc came at him. "Put it down," he said, wheezing.

Doc stood over him, watching.

Doc no longer looked like a young man.

He looked like a little boy. A frightened little boy.

In his hands, the saw and small hammer.

His lips were trembling, and his eyes crinkled up as he began weeping.

I'm safe. He's weak without her. He has nothing without her, Trey thought.

Doc Chilmark crouched beside his mother's body. He took it up, embracing her and kissing her lips and cheek and eyelids. "You promised you wouldn't leave me," Doc wept, pressing his face against his mother's bloodied throat. "You promised. Don't leave me. Put me in my cage. Put me in my cage."

CHAPTER FIFTY-FIVE

Doc couldn't see for his tears, and felt an awful ripping of something inside his body, as if his heart were breaking. He looked up to see if her shadow was there. If her spirit was nearby.

He was sure he saw it—it left her mouth as he kissed her—floating up like steam in the room.

She was there, her spirit, in the room with him.

And then he felt them coming.

He knew that they would once she was gone.

She was the only one who had kept the night fears back. And in this place, it was always night. She had protected him from them all his life, but now she was a shadow herself.

He could hear them making their smacking noises just beyond the door.

Doc glanced at Campbell and whispered, "Can you keep them out?"

But Trey had passed out, blood all around him where Doc had begun cutting at his scalp.

Nobody's gonna save you, the fears whispered within

Doc's mind. *We've been waiting a long, long time to find you. We knew she would go away someday. We knew you would be ours.*

"Please," he whispered, crawling over to Trey's body. He shook the man's arm, and slapped his face lightly. "Please wake up. Please stop them from getting me. I can't stand it. Please! Please stop them! They're crawling all over me! Stop them! Stop them!"

CHAPTER FIFTY-SIX

1

Trey opened his eyes. He looked straight up at the ceiling of the night cage, and beyond its mesh ceiling to the red light above.

He heard a noise—someone whispering near him.

He thought of Susan Hannafin. He needed to find her. He felt as if he were about to pass out again, and he took several deep breaths to fight it.

It took some effort, but he turned over onto his side, and then onto his stomach.

He couldn't quite stand, but he began putting one elbow in front of him and sliding forward. Then the other.

Doc lay shivering in a corner, clutching his dead mother's body to him like a rag doll. Scared out of his wits. "Please," he whispered. "They're crawling. I can feel them. They're gonna get inside me."

Trey reached for the pick, which lay a few feet from him. He crawled on his elbows for it. Got it. Then he began crawling slowly, almost snakelike toward the open door of the night cage.

He glanced back at Doc. "You tell me where she is. Where you put her. I'll make sure the night fears don't get you. But you better tell me. Or I'll cut you open and put them right in your skin."

So Doc told him where Susan Hannafin was, and then he told him where Jane Laymon had been kept. "The others are shadows now," Doc said, his eyes still wide with fear. "They're here now. Or they're headed for the light."

2

Trey tried to crawl forward, but had no more energy. He wondered if he was dying. He had wounds in his legs, his wrists had been slashed, and his side ached from another wound he could not remember getting. His scalp burned from the cut along it. He rolled over onto his back to breathe better. *Got to help Susan. Have to help her get out. Jane and Susan both. Gotta.*

"Susan? Susan!" he called out, but his voice was weak. He thought he heard a noise coming from the corridor that veered off to the left—the arm of the "crossroads" of the hallways where they began moving more and more into the territory of tunnels. He glanced over where he heard the tapping of footsteps, down into the dimly lit corridor with its peeling paint and broken wheelchairs propped beside the walls.

And then he thought he saw an angel. A woman outlined by a halo of light from the dim yellow glow of the distant tunnels.

Coming toward him.

Moving swiftly, as if she had wings.

3

Jane Laymon had finally broken through the old morgue's walls, using the kick technique. "I knocked my way out," Jane said to him. "Christ, Trey, you're really hurt bad."

"All right. All right," he said. "I thought you were dead."

"I thought we all were," Jane said. "Thank God you stuck around. Where's Blood Mary?"

"She's dead," Trey said, exhausted, full of an indescribable sorrow, unsure of his own sanity. "I killed her. With this." He let the long pick drop from his fingers.

"What about the other one?" Jane asked, reaching to lift Trey up.

"Down there," Trey murmured so softly that Jane had to put her ear near his mouth to hear him. "Down there." He tried to move his head so that it indicated the night cage. "He's scared to death that night fears are coming for him now. She was the only thing that protected him from them. That's what he thinks. Look, go get him. Susan . . . Dr. Hannafin . . . in a night cage. Over There. Brainard's dead. Lance is dead, too."

"Trey, I have never been so happy to see anyone in my life," Jane whispered, tears in her eyes.

"Me, too." Then he whispered something but didn't quite get it out.

"What?" she asked.

"The goodness of life itself. I knew it had to be here. Even down here," he said, but his voice was growing weaker. Trey felt himself blacking out.

As he drifted into unconsciousness, he thought he heard Susan Hannafin crying out for help from within one of the cages.

CHAPTER FIFTY-SEVEN

1

Jane checked Trey's pulse. It was weak, but there. He was alive. He'd get through it. She was certain.

She stood up and went back to the three doors to the night cages. "Dr. Hannafin? Susan?"

"Help me! Dear God, somebody help me!" came the scream that was not as loud on Jane's side as it was on Susan's. But Jane found the door, and using some of the tools that Mary Chilmark had left, she managed to pull the door open a quarter inch, and then Susan pushed it on the other side.

Jane held Hannafin close, while the psychiatrist wept against her shirt. "Look, we've got to get out. I'm going to need your help. It's a long way back upstairs."

"There's another way out," Hannafin said. "From down here, there's an exit that goes out into the residency halls. But . . . what if the fire . . ."

"I know you're feeling some form of shock," Jane

said. "But it's important. I need your help to get Trey out of here. We have to find one of the other ways."

Finally, Susan Hannafin said, "Please. Please. I don't know."

"Get a grip," Jane said. "No one knows we're way down here. We might as well be buried alive if we can't find the other exit."

"I know," a voice that sounded like a terrified little boy's came from one of the doorways. Doc Chilmark sat there, his knees drawn to his chest. "I know everything about this hospital. Since I was little. I know where every secret room is. I know where every doorway is."

"That guy gives me the creeps," Jane said under her breath. Then she stood and went over to make sure Doc Chilmark wasn't going to try anything. When she reached him, he had already bound his hands in restraints, and he'd locked hobbles on his ankles. "He said he'd protect me from them," Doc said, pointing with both wrists extended toward Trey. "I know how to get out. I'll take you out. There's nothing but shadows here."

2

The two women lifted Trey up between them, each bearing half his weight on a shoulder. Trey drifted in and out of consciousness, and as they went down one of the tunnels, Trey murmured, "It's all right. It's all right."

Doc Chilmark walked slowly in front of them. Jane

retrieved the gun that Bloody Mary had, and kept it pointed at Doc in case he was trying to trick them.

They passed other dark cells and rooms. Jane could not help glancing down them as they went—various cages and cells, and one long room off a tunnel full of metal beds. On the ceiling above, pipes of all shapes and sizes ran the length of the tunnel.

When they came near the end of the tunnel, where it veered off to the right and left, Doc kept them moving to the left, back toward the buildings of Darden State rather than away from them.

Finally, they came to a utility room, and within it, metal stairs up a towering stairwell.

A blue light wavered as if it were unstable near the ceiling above.

At the top step was another door, this one short and wide, and slightly ajar.

3

Jane Laymon, with all her strength, drew Trey up the steps, slowly, painstakingly, until they'd reached the low doorway at the top. She pushed through it and drew him out into the gardener's toolroom, within the residency building. Then out onto the lawn of Darden State.

The sky was dark with clouds—but rain came from them, rather than more black smoke.

Beautiful rain, Jane thought, as she drew Trey into it.

His eyes opened slightly as he looked up from her lap to the sky.

"It didn't reach us," Jane said. "The fire. It didn't reach us at all."

Trees along the edge of the grounds had been turned gray with ash, but the fire had not crossed the boulevard. The firemen and rescue workers had held it back—and something more, Jane considered, as she looked skyward.

Fate. Or God. Or Luck. Or Chance.

And then she remembered Trey's own phrase: *the goodness of life itself.*

Behind her, Susan emerged from the doorway, limping slightly.

It was a moment out of time—an uplift from the horrors of the day that they'd experienced. Each of them felt, within that moment, a sense of overcoming the worst that anyone could throw at them. In the next few seconds, that might be gone, without any of them realizing why it had touched them and then passed.

But in its touch—of rising from the darkness into ordinary daylight, ordinary rain—there was a spark of something that would never leave them even in the worst hours of their existence.

Except for Doc Chilmark.

For him, the night fears always came back.

EPILOGUE

1

His first night home after his release from the hospital, Trey lay in bed with his wife, and held her so much that she nearly had to push him away just to breathe.

"I'm sorry," he said.

"It's okay. After what you went through . . ."

"I want the baby."

"Oh."

"Do you?" he asked.

She nodded. "I guess it just was such a shock to find out. But I do. I'm just scared to have a baby this late. All the things we have to go through, what's going to happen with my work. What'll happen with the other kids, and how old we'll be when the baby's eighteen, and well, all the stuff you think about."

Trey reached to her and drew her back to him. "I want the baby because I want to know that something good can come into the world," he said. "I want us to be the kinds of parents who raise kids who have purpose. Who get help when they need it. Who allow their kids to be productive and happy. Who protect them when we can."

She kissed him on the neck. "That's why I married you. Because you're a good man."

"There are plenty of good men out there," he whispered.

"None like you," she said.

"There's so much bad in the world," he said. "I don't even like thinking about it. Or our kids—how they'll be affected by it."

"You see too much bad," Carly said.

"I do. Now and then, I do. This family keeps me sane," he said, trying to block out the memory of what he'd seen beneath Darden State. "You make me think about what's good." He began kissing her, and he never wanted to stop.

2

Quentin "Doc" Chilmark was given a new cage as part of his therapy in Darden State. It was not quite a dog crate, but simply a large box. He slept in it at night, but with all the lights on in his room, which had gotten smaller and had no view at all.

He lay in his straitjacket at night, his eyes wide open, listening to the shadows that came and went, talking of death and of heaven. And sometimes the dead girl came to him, too, and sat with him in the cage and told him that she was happy to have made a friend, because she had been so lonely when she'd been alive.

But sometimes, she didn't come.

Sometimes he felt the crawling fears moving toward him, coming for him just as he fought off sleep.

Sometimes they spoke with his mother's voice.

3

Within three weeks, much of the underground to Darden State was sealed up. The entrances in various underground buildings were closed off with concrete, and the doorway in the canteen of Ward D was refitted with a reinforced steel door that only opened with specific identification cards in a bar-code-like device. An administrative memo circulated about the need for a cleaning crew to go into the two levels beneath Darden State and clear out any material, as well as to seal rooms individually, particularly the old night cages on the lowest level.

At Darden, a budget was drawn up within six months of meetings of several directors and the board itself, and so it was put to the state to provide three million dollars for the project to clear out the underground once and for all.

Nothing came of this, and the hospital ran as it always did, and always would.

Aboveground, several new patients were admitted. There were staff reassignments. Trey Campbell returned to work once he'd recuperated from his injuries completely. Dr. Susan Hannafin sold a second book about her time at Darden State, called *Inside the Night Cage: The American Asylum and the Mind's Secret Places*, although she resigned from her position and went into private practice in San Diego. When Trey and Carly Campbell's son was born in the summer, his wife suggested they name the boy "Jim," and Trey felt that was a damn good name, if you asked him.